"Regressions **is a riveting tale of love echoing across the chasm of multiple lives and realities. It ricochets through past, present and future, venturing into worlds dancing at the edge of consciousness. To go on this journey is to enter the many layered mysteries of time while exploring the often-confounding nuances of the heart. Masterfully rendered in a style that is at once revealing and elusive, it haunts the reader like the evaporating wisps of last night's dream. Mark William Allard is a magnificent storyteller!"**

-Paul Rademacher, author of *A Spiritual Hitchhiker's Guide to the Universe: Travel Tips for the Spiritually Perplexed*

"Thought-provoking and beautifully written, ***Regressions*** **is a treasure trove of significant messages and authentic experiences. It led me on a journey of great depth, vividness, and fascinating detail that equally satisfied both mind and heart!"**

-Alishia M. Alibhai, Ph.D. Social Psychologist, Past Life Coach & Soul Coach

"Regressions **is a masterpiece, weaving threads of our dreams with poetry, sparking collective memories of lives past and those to come. Mark William Allard has an incredible gift.** ***Regressions*** **escorted me through the ages and brought me to the now moment, where we can all learn and grow."**

-Carole M. Friesen, contributing author of the Amazon bestseller, *Succeeding In Spite Of Everything*

"Regressions **reads like a half-awake journal, deftly jumping time and space, from location to physical sensation to forgotten emotion; from lost dreams to snapshot memories. The best way to read this novel, if only one could, would be to take in every word and line simultaneously and ingest it as a whole."**

-Tona Ohama, Singer/Songwriter

“An eloquently written emotional account of a young man’s slip into altered states of consciousness. Exciting and magical in tone, layered generously with new spiritual insights and philosophical gems, *Regressions* is an intelligent and credible version of the purpose of our lives in the physical realm and subsequent growth found in our life between lives. Amidst a labyrinth of mystical breathtaking adventures and oozing with honesty, the author pulled me into my own imagination, tugged at my heart strings and shed light on the cyclical nature of patterns which keep us from moving through life’s challenges. Allard writes with a style that puts me in mind of James Redfield’s The *Celestine Prophecy.* I found myself enveloped in a tranquil energy that transported me outside of time and space to a place far more real. If *Regressions* does not find itself high upon the best sellers list, then I am no judge of literature. I loved it! I highly recommend it!”

-Deborah Rees, founder of Accolade Academy of Psychic & Mediumistic Studies

“In Regressions, Mark has found his message. He is living it and now he wants us to join him there in the space where the past is toothless, where authentic love can be discovered and where friends can be human. I, for one, am eager to meet him there; but mostly I’m thrilled Mark is leading the charge.”

-Les Mottosky, from the After Word

“*Regressions* is a fantastical and magical story that pulls the reader through the deep wisdom of life, truth, and what it means to be human - and what it means to be something else all together. Giving us clarifying piñatas filled with truth and yet even more questions, *Regressions* pushes us forward in our own journeys. The tale is damn vulnerable, generous and humble. Ridiculously great writing. I am so moved. I learned so much! I am overwhelmed with gratitude.This is the kind of book I’ve searched years for. Mark Allard, thank you for the many gifts you’ve given us all with *Regressions.*”

-Jay Baydala, founder of UEnd:Poverty

Regressions

The Lengths People Will Go to Discover Authentic Love

Mark Allard

Balboa Press books may be ordered through booksellers or by contacting:

Balboa Press
A Division of Hay House
1663 Liberty Drive
Bloomington, IN 47403
www.balboapress.com
1-(877) 407-4847

ISBN: 978-1-4525-5612-3 (sc)
ISBN: 978-1-4525-5613-0 (hc)
ISBN: 978-1-4525-5614-7 (e)

Library of Congress Control Number: 2012913584

Printed in the United States of America

Balboa Press rev. date: 08/30/2012

For Taylor, thanks

**If it's true that we create our own reality,
how much do I love myself for creating you?**

Contents

Regressions:
A Meditation on Finding Your Authentic Voice

In an age overwrought with intellect and reason, *Regressions* comes to us as an antidote to the rational mind; a reminder of something we've always known but have long forgotten.

Written in the symbolic language of the heart, *Regressions* invites us to explore the possibilities of our potential to imagine and create the story of our lives.

In a tone of warmth and familiarity—the tone of internal dialogue, we discover an expression of truths that lie at the centre of our human experience. The most intimate regions of ourselves are confronted with a touching degree of reassurance and wisdom. This form of honesty and insight resonates in the heart and forces the reader to live there. You are challenged to consider this very moment, regressing within yourself to a place of pure vulnerability, where your authentic voice resides.

Like the workings of a dream, the author uses the imagery of material experience as a mirror reflecting the world of the spirit.

Recognizing the limitations of language to describe the inner world of nature, a new format of writing was necessary to capture this state of impermanence. Thus the narrative is structured as a series of archetypal themes that appear at seemingly random intervals.

Despite the rational mind's attempt to neatly organize and file these away, *Regressions* offers a fluidity of ideas that guide the reader gracefully through each transition back to the centre. As your mind floats through landscapes of true beauty and emotion it becomes clear that your own personal dialogue and associations are just as powerful and relevant as the content within the pages.

As quickly as you settle into a new scene you are led back out again; through dream regions of fantasy, love, memories, death and beyond—

each scene a cosmic breath, always returning to that place of origin, refreshed with new experience. *Regressions* is a work that reaches far beyond the realm of story telling. It is a return to an ancient form of spiritual philosophy; a tool to assist the workings of the soul; the first step of realignment to the natural order of being—living through your authentic voice.

Do you have the courage to speak your truth?

Benjamin Pearson, July 2012

Acknowledgements

Thanks to everyone who read *Regressions* from its infant stages to the final draft and provided feedback, encouragement, and proofreading.

Dr. Alisha M. Alibhai and the community at Divine Bliss.

Mom and Dad for your constant support.

Les Mottosky, for enhancing the vision.

Mustapha Khalil for endless perspective.

Sasha Popove for the book trailer.

An amazing team at VISCERAL MFI.

The Monroe Institute.

Taylor—my princess, for taking
this journey with me.

Introduction

I have known Mark W. Allard since moving into an old historic building on Stephen Avenue in downtown Calgary, where we live as neighbours.

From our first conversation, it was apparent to me that Mark has many creative talents. It didn't take many of our impromptu encounters to discover his appreciation for the unseen.

It is rare to have personally relevant conversation on a deeper level with others, yet every conversation we have had has remained consistent. They start with sharing a moment or key experience, which—on its own, appears mundane on the surface and common to anyone, but then something remarkable would happen. He would share a perspective which extended to various, more 'abstract' subjects such as world religions, politics, history (and how it was written), economics, or any number of social sciences that served as drivers for inter and intrapersonal behaviours. Our conversations would then end with a lovely denouement which applied the new insights we had generated to the next moment, day, month, or year. I found the process created anticipation for how these new insights would affect my life and, ultimately, our next conversation.

We've all been involved in conversation which drone on and on. Sometimes they touch on meaning, but too often leave us feeling a lack of fulfillment. How can we have deeper and more meaningful connections with everyone in our lives without describing too much detail, yet still exchanging complex ideas? The answer would surely impact all of my relationships—from co-workers and family, to friends and lovers.

Over breakfast one morning, we concluded that stories are a key instrument for introducing universally relatable ideas into the most personal of relationships, and in a reasonable amount of time.

How does one go about writing stories that others can understand and still find entertaining? By speaking the language of the heart. This is something *Regressions* manages to do with ease.

My conversations with Mark over the last year have allowed me to take small journeys which defy space and time into Mark's life and him into mine, yet they only scratched the surface of what I was discovering at the time. Not until I read the first draft of *Regressions* did I realize that each one of our conversations was a form of regression into Marks own life—a journey through the timestreams into universal consciousness, to arrive at a place we can all relate to, emotion.

Regressions manages to weave the unenviable events of existence into a fabric of reality that is nothing less than the sensation of home.

Regressions contains a multitude of facets. Each contains a story which stands on its own. Each contains a new insight that, when observed together, resonates a beauty which is easily and pleasantly shared but hard to describe.

Much like a diamond, *Regressions* charts a course through his-story, and we are invited into these parallel worlds of shared reality.

I expect that as you travel through *Regressions*, you will also discover how your own life is a diamond, uniquely yours, worthy of gratitude and appreciation.

Mustapha Khalil July 2012

INITIATION

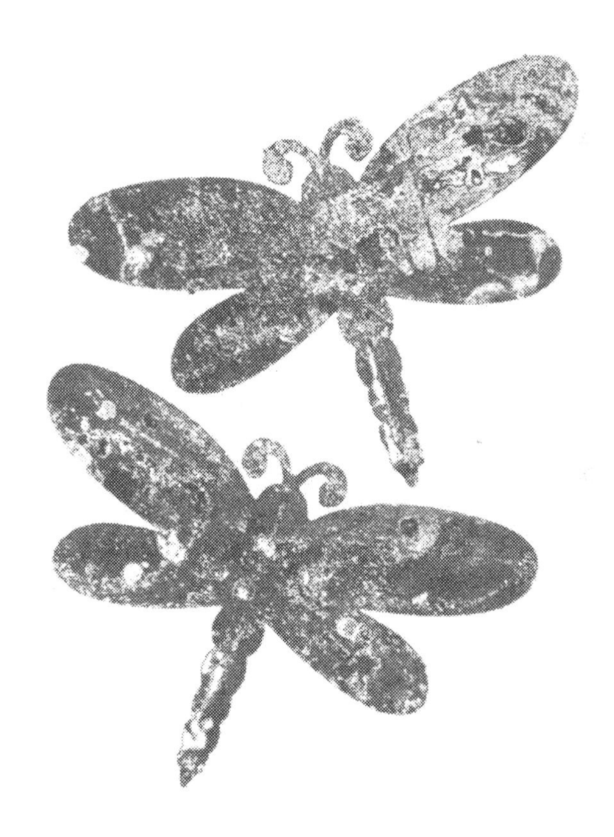

If I find in myself a desire which no experience in this world can satisfy, the most probable explanation is that I was made for another world.

C.S. Lewis

SERGEANT

The Killing Options

"You can feel the sun on your skin like it's burning impressions into you." This is how he would begin writing, if he survived.

The jungle is thick, though its canopy does little to offer relief from the sun. Heat seems to rise off the ground and even the plants are prone to sweating.
The jungle is a world of its own. Smells are different. Taste is unnatural. Hearing becomes amplified, sight—diminished. Touch is a lifeline.
Creation makes a gesture of empathy towards the fools who trespass here, knowing well the inevitable destruction they must pay as the toll for entering this place.
The cost is not the same for everyone. Some pay immediately, with their life or limbs or health. Others think they got out easy, only to find themselves stalked by cyclical demons of paranoia and sabotage through countless attempts at rebuilding life away from this place.
The jungle is a jealous lover. If she can't have you, she won't let anyone.

About 100 feet from where you stand is the ocean, maybe 200 feet. It doesn't matter what direction, just pick one. The important thing is not to doubt yourself. Whatever pops into your mind ought to be right.
The waves crash on themselves, stretching their wake onto white sands, like a deceptive picture implying paradise.
That thought is not in the present. It is something you are imagining—maybe even remembering, yet somehow you know that what you are seeing in your mind's eye is *that* beach—the one two hundred feet away, with crystal blue water washing up polished lava rocks on a sun soaked mirage of tranquility, until the tide once again relocates them.

The sound of a bird brings you back. Was it a bird at the beach, one from the jungle, or did it resonate from a distant memory? It is hard to tell and makes little difference. You are back. Back to the heat and the smell of your own sweat and the relief that comes with knowing the journey has to end, sometime. The tide deposited you here. The crashing waves in the distance taunt, "you can never go back." And you know it is true. The white sand as forbidden as a virgin, the water beyond—leading anywhere, may just as well be across a great chasm for which no bridge exists to take you to the other side. Within that chasm lie booby traps and landmines and snakes and killing options. There are neither trees big enough nor vines long to help you cross over. Besides, you know which direction you need to keep walking.

As if responding to the very thought in your head, the trees seem to bend at eye level, revealing a hill in the distance. It is further in front of you than the ocean is behind, and as quickly as you glimpse your destination the trees resume their original shape. There is no path for you. You must forge your own through trees that bend and sweating plants and ground that gives off heat.

It could take hours, and life—especially life in the jungle, rarely follows a straight line, but somehow you know that you will be there before the sun sets.

NOGWAL

Self Awareness

You are in the dark. You try hard to picture something—anything; a tree, moss, rocks, running water. You are not even able to do that. What is happening? You look around you. You look down at your hands and can't even see them, but you can feel them. You form a fist, then stretch your fingers wide. If you can *feel* your hands moving but not see them, you must be blind or in the dark.
The physical you—the one with flesh and bones, is still alive. It's a place to start. At least you aren't dead.

The sensation of awareness travels up from your hands, through your arms and shoulders, before emptying into your chest. You become aware of your breath; the rhythmic inhale and exhale.
Now you are certain you are really here, surrounded by darkness.
But where is here? You have no memory of arriving in this dark place.

How are you feeling? *Scared. Panicked.* The words come fast and effortlessly.
What is your life's purpose? *Escape.*

SERGEANT

Clean Sweep

You look down at your feet.
I am in the jungle. My boots are heavy, as if weighed down with stones. Perhaps this is just the weight of my tired legs. Suddenly the boots are gone and you can see your golden brown feet walking effortlessly through the thick underbrush.
Boots are back on. A hill is in front of me. The destination.

I begin to see things unfold like I am watching a silent film; one I have already seen, which removes the suspense of it all. I am an observer, watching my alternate self experience, but unable to *feel* it.

You are holding a book. A kind of encyclopaedia of animals. When I reach the snakes, I am so afraid; I can't even touch the pictures. With the tip of my finger I turn the page over. It would be better if there was something between me and the pages. I don't want to accidentally come into contact with the pictures. My touch is all that is required to awaken these frozen serpents.

I feel like I have been abandoned. The jungle is hot and my clothes are sticky. Why are you here alone? What happened to everyone? I can't remember, but I feel like I have been misjudged.
I see something red in the trees. Maybe it is a bird. I keep walking.

Family vacation. You are six or seven? I am sitting in the sand with some toys. As the water rolls in I look up. A snake emerges from the water and heads straight towards me. You are frozen. Will it end like this? I know what snakes can do.
A few feet in front of me it rears up, standing within its scaled cocoon. It's tongue hisses at me. Our eyes meet.

Memories-like shards of ice on a still pond that have shattered. The broken pieces have begun to drift away. I must bring them back. I must do this before it's too late. If I could collect the pieces, I could reform a surface that would allow me to see my own reflection. For now, all I see are fragments.

Red in the trees. Boots on. Boots off. What am I missing?
It feels like I have been left here. *Abandonment.*
I hear a voice sing to me—the memory of some childs lullaby I have forgotten.
What am I running from? Who have I abandoned? Who or what am I running *to*?

I escape from the beach. I am crying and screaming because I am so afraid. My body is vibrating. I run to where my parents and their friends are, but no one will believe me. They all think you are lying, as if I even want their attention. I wouldn't have mentioned it but you are afraid, and fear makes people do unstable things.
You don't believe me! I saw a snake. Why does no one ever believe me? Why do they always think I am lying? Can't they see what they are doing to me? I will grow up and doubt myself, sheltering what I really think and feel because if I express myself people will misinterpret me. They will think I am lying. Why can't they see this?

It came out of the water and headed straight for me. It stood in its scaled cocoon and our eyes met. I don't know why it stopped. I don't know why it let me go. Maybe because not being believed is worse.
I am not a liar. Why won't you believe me? Is this how it will end?

When I was ten there was a stairway in my closet. No more than a dozen narrow steps led up towards the attic. What existed beyond that door filled me with as much excitement as it did trepidation. It wasn't just an attic, it was a way out. It was change.
What if that world turned out to be more horrible than the one I already knew? I didn't want to be stuck there. What if opening that door meant things would never be the same?
I would hate to discover cobwebs and mothballs. I think that would be a worse fate than never opening it at all. Sometimes the hope of a thing is better than an absolute.

You think about this entirely too much. My logic begins to question if the door is not there to be opened, but guarded. Perhaps it is your responsibility to make sure the door stays closed. Maybe this is why you were put here.
I think I am just going to wait. In an emergency, it won't matter if it is the right thing to do or not. It won't matter if I find cobwebs and mothballs. The only thing that will matter is that I have an escape.

I have no memories of ever opening the attic door, though I find it hard to accept that I never tried.
Two years we lived in that house. Perhaps those memories were wiped away.
I believe in that kind of thing. I believe our higher self works with the body to create the circumstances we call life. It does this because there is a point to us being here. *Something we have forgotten.* The events of life are just exercises in remembering. The catch is, what doesn't make you stronger kills you.

It's a temporary solution—losing memories. It does some good in the short term, but no one can outrun the toll, not even by denying

the consequences of choices or downplaying their relevance. Choice becomes us. YOU are the change you are looking for.
Memories are a lot like dreams that way. The ones that I forget are—no doubt, the most significant.

I must be getting close now. The sun is about to set and I know I will arrive before then. The jungle is so thick it is hard to tell how close I am or how far I've come.

NOGWAL

Mistaken For Dead

A terrifying thought occurs to me. What if I am in a wooden box, deep in the ground? I once read about a casket that was designed with a kind of pipe leading to the surface to provide air for someone in this very situation.
I suppose you would have a few days of screaming before your body resigned itself to die; hopefully before your stomach began eating itself.
I believe that kind of thing happens—that we can make a decision and just say, "I'm done," and the darkness closes in. It's like suicide without ever pulling the trigger.
The longer you lie here, the harder it becomes to have any hope that I will be saved.

I can only imagine the oxygen casket was designed because someone was buried alive and survived the ordeal. What a thought. Imagine being that guy?
Something must have been terribly wrong with his body to go into shut down mode—enough that he was mistaken for dead. Then to wake up, find yourself in the dark, come to the conclusion that you are buried and dig yourself out—that's got to change you. It would change everything. Every perspective would be re-evaluated. Every belief system would be challenged.
Whoever that guy was—who inspired the ultimate insurance policy against premature burial, they must have worshipped him. How would he ever fully resolve that he had not been legitimately dead? That no mistake had been made? That some greater force had not chosen to resurrect him for some great purpose?

The sheer panic of waking up in darkness and clawing your way to emancipated freedom—fingers bleeding and caked with blood and splinters, this has got to be significant.
Why was he required to dig himself out of the ground, as though it were essential to the process of resurrection; a mandatory requirement?
What strange and sympathetic magic orchestrates this kind of event?

It's not everyone who comes back from the dead. By the time they figured it out—if they did, that he was just like the rest of them, the truth would have become irrelevant. He was a *God of the New World.*

THE ONE THEY CALL THE VISION

A Place I Visit With My Eyes Closed

It is the sensation of moving very quickly. I am flying above fields towards the Glenn.
I descend through a canopy of trees that shield the magic contained within this ancient place. The fairy forest, she calls it.
Something is different this time. The colors are more vibrant. This place is more alive and more intimidating in its stillness.
It is snowing lightly. All of the green is peppered with glistening white.

I picture myself here with her in a different time. I am standing in the trunk of a tree that is split down the center, forming a kind of archway. She calls this the doorway for faeries to enter our world.
These memories are like dreams to me. A place I visit with my eyes closed.

As the branches part, I see a body lying in the snow. His arms are spread open like the ascending Christ. His black hair is wet and the melting snow gives it shine. He wears furs wrapped around his body. It looks like a blanket beneath him.
I come to realize that the body lying in the snow is me. I can't explain how I am watching myself or how I was floating through the air and descending through the trees. I don't know where I was coming from but the body I see belongs to me. The memories I have belong to me, and by me I mean *that* body, and *this* essence.

It has been such a long journey. I have been away from home for so long.

Your eyes flutter in the falling snow. My body is cold but there are warm spots. Why are you lying here? Why did I come here?
As quickly as you ask, I find myself transported.

SERGEANT

The Switch

Imagination is a word grownups use to imply pretending, but only because they have forgotten what it's like. I don't pretend. I create worlds.

I often wonder if that is why I got electrocuted. Did I mention that? It happened when I was eleven. My body was bouncing off the floor. It was that bad. I could have died. Instead I lost my childhood.

It seems entirely possible to me that I was electrocuted because I saw too much. I saw things I needed to see at the time, and then needed to forget until the time was right to remember. I believe that time is now.

Sometimes I think parents have this idea that imagination works like a switch, as though it can be turned on and off; convenient when you send your children away to play, inconvenient when you are trying to sleep and they are screaming about people in their room with machine guns and snakes all over the floor.

Before I was electrocuted, I saw a lot of things differently; people and animals and sickness. I could see a headache and pull it out like a string.

Something is travelling above me. I can hear it. I look up but can't tell what it is through the thickness of the trees. Occasionally its shadow descends but disappears and it is moving too fast for me to make out its shape.

It makes a sound like the banging of a drum, and another—a humming. To be honest, I find it comforting. I don't feel so lonely.

CONQUERER

Footsteps Of Our History

I am at the top of a hill. Beside me is some kind of stone monument. It looks like a navigational instrument, used to tell the distance of things.
Below me is a village on the coast.

About a mile into the icy waters, the sea has spit up a black rock castle. Its towers stand in rebellion to the violent waters around it, and the role it must play. Swarms of fowl converge on this place, claiming it as their own.
I wonder if all creatures see creation unfold the same way? I think they must. We are all just trying to survive. We are all just doing what we know how to do. We have all seen too much blood and suffering.
Why am I here?

Time reverses. I am not in my body. My physical body lies in the Glenn far away from here; the snow falling gently on my face. I sense the wolf nearby and the heat from between my legs. I am a ghost in these memories, haunting myself. Time is becoming irrelevant.

I am climbing the hill with *my love*. She seems uncomfortable. I don't trust her complaints. She just wants attention. It is important that she give birth here. This is my only concern.
Our child will be a *God of the New World*. We shall return to my home in the north, avenge my brother's death, and lead our people to victory.
I ignore her complaints. We must make it to the top. She will earn no sympathy from me, today.

With the tilt of my head I watch this scenario repeat itself. In a different time and details have changed. We are climbing the same hill. Marching in the footsteps of our history. Things look different, somehow. The colors have faded and she bears no child, but my scorn is the same. I want to reach the top. It is the only thing that matters—as if this act of penance will heal the wounds that have surfaced before the pain.

I am surprised to see the navigational instrument still here. It has weathered.
I look out at the icy waters of Oceans Gate. I see the black rock castle—towering out of the sea in rebellion.
Below me is the village, though it looks strange. It is not how I remember. It *feels* strange. The memories I have associated with this place are jumbled. It looks modern but is somehow less advanced.
I remember watching Sinister burn to the ground. The village below me is a recycled version from my memories—as if creation took the easy way out.
I contemplate going down and exploring, but am drawn back to *my love.*
Two versions of this scene play side by side. I need only to tilt my head slightly to watch the other.

While out of the body, I retain all the memories I have collected from these alternate experiences. It is only inside the human suit that I am prone to forget. With these memories, I am forming a kind of map that will help me navigate my way through the timestreams; help me understand why this happening and perhaps allow me to stop this. Or change things. Things like outcomes not yet absolute.

We have reached the top. Am I ready to watch this again?
The sky has grown dark and she is about to give birth. We find shelter in the place the shepherds have built for the windy, rainy nights. She is crying out. I hear the child. Something is happening that sends my body into shivers. Tiny orbs of bright light surround us and float away. The baby is gone.

How did this begin?

WARRIOR

PRIVEDEN

It is early. The plan is to leave while everyone is sleeping. I sneak out without making a sound. In the fields, the playfulness of GOEL heightens the expectation of adventure.
For a moment I feel as if I have left my body—mysteriously drawn back to memories from an earlier time, held captive on the very earth I walk.
We were at war. This field was a battleground. Many died around me. Many have died in countless battles for survival. At such times, men are granted the blessing of ruthlessness. It is a grace we give one another to fight long and hard and fearlessly. We take the enemy—dead or alive, and castrate them. We bury them standing up, allowing just one of their hands to reach out of the ground. In that hand we place their genitals. Were they unfortunate enough to be buried alive, when they breathe their last, the muscles of their hand atrophy an eternal hold on their lost manhood, a warning to all who come against us that a similar fate awaits them. A reminder to us that we are all monsters.

I am back in my body; back to the new morning and the calm stillness. Back to leaving the house before anyone is awake and moving slowly across these fields of my home.
I don't know how long it will be until I return so I do not rush. GOEL and I take our time. This landscape is burned into my memory. I just want to take it all in one last time.

Most of the arms are no longer visible. The long winter and the wild beasts have taken care of that. It's a costly omen, promising the return of war. Yet still I leave this place?

One cannot fight forever. Real change will happen with real sacrifice. I am still too young and naive to fully understand this, but for now I must go. I must heal myself before I am eaten alive from the inside. Something greater awaits me to account for this favour.

If you look close, you can see bones, and bodies buried underneath.

CONQUERER

Oceans Gate

When we lost the baby, I blamed you. I cursed God. I loved you and I left you on the mountain.
I saw the end of my days as I watched life escape from your eyes. There was nothing I could do to save you.
I fled to Oceans Gate. The icy waters break on the beach. I remember this place so well. The sand wrapping around my feet like claws and the resignation between my toes as every step led me closer to home.
I imagine holding you again—the way I did only days ago. I held you on the nearby rocks.
How differently things were then. How quickly they have changed.
All I ever wanted was for my life to make sense; for some event to explain the meaning behind all the pain I have experienced.
I thought this was the event. I suppose it is, but this is not the outcome I anticipated. I lack an explanation, and long for answers to questions I am unsure how to ask.

"I have never felt more in love with you than I do now. From that first moment I fell into your eyes, I was transported into a kind of completeness; a love I had waited stubbornly for.
In you I saw someone just as willing to return the love I wanted to give. We calibrated one another. You transformed my restless soul into calm.
All our hopes and desires and lusts awaken at night.
Apart, we were half moons. Tonight, my love, we will be a full moon once again."

You are crying and you step into the icy waters, with joyful resignation between my toes.

NAVIGATOR

MADE OUT OF NOTHING

When I was a child, I remember trying to walk on water. It seemed like it should come quite naturally, after all, Jesus did it, and he did say that those who come after him will do even greater things than he.
I guess that was written down by one of his followers; scribbled into a notebook or something.
How absurd that we imagine this. That never happened. No one followed Jesus around writing down his words.

We believe a lot of things we are told as children—and with a little imagination, we grow up wrapped and bound in a story of ourselves others have told us, never knowing our personal truth; unable to express our own essence.

The only reason we discard dreams is because we wake up and tell ourselves it was a dream. The only reason we discard Santa Claus is because someone told us that he didn't exist.
The only reason we discard identity is because we have been trained to believe others will provide it for us, like a nickname.

CONQUERER

GOLGOTHA

I am cold and wet. The black rock castle does little to shelter me from the wind, but I manage to find a cleft in the rocks to hide myself. I shouldn't be here. I am not sure how I arrived. Did I walk across the water? Was I carried here?
Far in the distance—across the raging waters that divide my new prison from the world I grew to despise, I see the hilltop with the navigational instrument on the top and the little stone shelter built by the sheppard's.
I watch tiny orbs float upwards and I become aware that what I am watching is happening in the present; that at this very moment, my love is about to breathe her last breath and I am falling into all the life in her eyes one last time.
I don't know how this is happening or why I am here and how I survived. I don't know much but, oh my, does this change things.

I close my eyes and journey the timestreams. I come to understand her resistance to the climb, as if it were her personal Golgotha. I suppose it was, many times over, and still is.

Everything we have done is a reflection of what we are doing. It's all happening now. If I can learn more about this I can change things. I can release myself from the prison of my own making—alone and cold on a black rock castle, spit up in rebellion. I will save *my love* and our *God of the New World*. We will restore Priveden to her majesty.
I allow myself to remember. Further back, to when we are walking through the Glenn.

"You are leading me where the faeries live," she says. ""Which way do we walk?"

There are two paths ahead of us. To the left, the path inclines into the trees. To my right, it descends.

Resisting logic, I make my decision based on instinct; intuition. *I have been here before.* And then I see it. One of the paths seems brighter. A faint hue surrounding the leaves, growing in intensity.

"This is the path I choose."

She smiles. I know I have made the right choice.

We walk up the hill, and the path turns sharply before it descends into a clearing. There are great trees here—mighty trees whose roots have separated at the bottom, providing a natural archway. You can walk through these trees, or stand *in* them.

"This is how the faeries enter our world," she tells me.

I stand inside the hollow of the tree and look up, into the endless spiral of trunk that leads to a fine point I cannot see. How long I stand here I can't say. The next thing I remember is the chapel. This is where we are to be married. We are hovering above it—the chapel I have come to build. This is why I left Priveden. There is magic here and I love you.

If I could learn to silence the chatter of logic—the voice of my ego, I could recall the memories inside me. It's pride that prevents me from learning.

Sometimes, when the moment comes to be extrordinary, I choose to forget because extrordinary would mean change. Change is like a door in your closet. You just don't know what you are going to get if you open it.

THE ISLAND

Overboard

You are lying in a wooden boat floating on the ocean.
There is no one else with you. I don't know what happened to them. *Try and remember.*
I feel as if they should be here or were here, but for some reason I have been abandoned.
The ocean rocks the boat mercilessly. Perhaps they fell overboard.
The dense fog adds a layer of eerie to the situation. I can't see a thing. Rocks could be lying in wait or beasts swimming alongside. Land could be right in front of me or months away.
I don't know anything except there is much I don't know.

The fog responds to my turmoil and starts to thin. The raging waters subside. The sun is out now and the fog is entirely gone.
I notice land less than a mile away. The ocean is so calm. I consider stepping from the boat onto the crystal blue surface; walking the rest of the way to land.
The closer in I drift, the more the island looks strange to me. Instead of sharp rocks, there is white sand. Beyond that, trees unlike any I have seen. They are thick and dense and full of life. Something red moves in the trees.
I must have drifted off course. Either that or I am dead and this is some kind of weigh station.
There are no oars in the boat so I kneel down and paddle with my arms. The water is warm, yet refreshing.
When I can see the floor beneath the water, I jump out of the boat and walk the rest of the way in.

I have made a fire and am sitting on the white sandy beach, surrounded by polished stones carried in and out with the tide. I have been here for hours, trying to decide what to do. I feel like I am waiting for someone-someone to explain explain this to me; for it all to make sense. I would even settle for a wraith to escort me to hell.

NOGWAL

The Simplest Of Questions

What if I am at the morgue in one of those steel drawers? Someone made a mistake and put me in here because they thought I was dead. It would be better than being buried alive. Then again, things have changed. Premature burial isn't an option anymore. They cut people up now before they bury them. They drain your blood. It makes the whole oxygen casket thing irrelevant.

If I haven't been cut up yet, then someone will eventually open the door and free me. If they have, then I am already dead, and I'm pretty sure that because I am even questioning if I am dead, makes it a good bet that I'm not. Dead people who hang around generally don't know they are dead.

I clench my fingers into a fist. These fingers of mine—judgement, spiritual, ambition and social. They're all snug into the heart of my hand. My will wraps around them like a blanket.

I lie here with all the peace and calm and panic you could imagine. Does that even make sense? To be honest, nothing makes any sense to me and all I want is for this to make sense.

THE ONE THEY CALL THE VISION

The Biggest Weakness

I am floating above the Glenn, trying hard to remember what I have forgotten.
Descending through the trees. My body lying in the snow. I could go inside it, but I fear I may become trapped and I must figure this out. Somewhere out here—wherever here is, are the answers I am looking for. Or perhaps there are no answers, just a lot of riddles.
There are things you can do in spirit that are not possible in a physical body. Is this what I am now, spirit? I don't even know the answer to the simplest of questions.

I see myself as a little boy in front of our house. It is winter and you have built a snow fort in the front yard. It's fortified like a castle, built in rebellion. I sit on the top level and admire the work you have put into this.
I am afraid to crawl through the tunnels I have built. Building them was no problem but crawling through them now, I just can't do. The fort could collapse and I would be trapped inside. I don't want to die that way.

I stand in my father's study. There is a large safe in the corner that has been here since we moved in. The owners probably left it because it is awkward and heavy. I imagine it is full of money and precious things. You sneak in the study and pray to Jesus to help you unlock the safe. Wouldn't everyone be proud, especially if you discovered enough

money in there to move far away and then mom wouldn't have to work anymore?
It is unnerving to watch myself. It feels voyeuristic; consciousness acting like a ghost observing the physical shell of you.

I have a theory. About dreams. Daydreams to. When we sleep our consciousness leaves us to gather information from what is happening in the alternates-those multiple versions of us somewhere in the multiverse; within the timestreams. Information that could be useful in our present reality. And when it does, those versions travel to the body we left behind, and explore, learning the memories contained within that body.
Our bodies store memories in their tissue. It's not as complex as it sounds. I am just not explaining it well.
Consciousness shares memories with our alternate selves. Our brain is constantly processing the information of our shared consciousness.
The same consciousness that allows the sperm and the egg to form a baby is the same consciousness we replace with logic. Logic tries to filter what information is relevant—what can serve us in this life and what should just be discarded.
I don't think my logic is an adequate judge.

The only form of ownership is time. It is a third dimension experience. From within the timestreams, time—as we understand it, is irrelevant. It is entirely possible that alternate realities are happening simultaneously. If so, my decisions in this present reality could affect what happens in others. That kind of adds a new level of responsibility to my decisions. Something about the darkness is helping me remember.

You see yourself standing in my room—in front of the closet with the staircase inside, not sure if you want to proceed further.
The biggest weakness is me.

GOEL

The Wolf

His breath changes. That subtle change is my alarm clock. This is how I am always awake before him.
We have been together since we were both young. I know everything about him. I have studied his behaviour and we communicate with the simplest of looks and gestures. We have played together; we have killed together. There is nothing I would not do for him.
I can tell how he is feeling by the fluctuation in his voice. Lately, he seems distressed. I have watched him prepare for a journey. The journey starts this morning. I can feel it. I know it.
He steps out of bed more quietly than usual. He doesn't want to wake anyone. He dresses and I follow him out of the bedroom where he collects some provisions.

He hesitates at the door. This has been a hard decision for him. He thinks he is sneaking away without anyone knowing but his mother is awake. She studies him in her own way and knows things about him without ever hearing him speak. She knew this day was coming, and has been rising early for the last week. When she heard us through her door, it sent a shiver through her. She is worried. Not just for him, but for her and the rest of the family.

He hates his father. He blames him for making poor decisions that have continually led them to war. His brother is dead.
We blame his father.
When his brother died, his father changed. He began to spend a lot of time alone drinking wine and getting angry and making bad decisions.

One time they were fighting. They used their swords. It didn't start out as a battle, but it became one. I wished he would kill his father. They were both determined to prove something.
His brother would have made good decisions that would save the family more bloodshed. His brother is gone and he is resenting his mother more and more for tolerating his father. She should confront him; tell him he is making bad decisions.
She is too compliant. He knows because she tells him things privately, and he does not understand why people stay in these situations, as though bound to live out a single version of fate.
I would kill his father. I have thought about it. Then we wouldn't have to go on this journey. He wouldn't have to leave his sister. They are very close and she is slowly going mad.
Sometimes I wonder if the whole point of their life is conflict. It seems that way.

Last night we dreamed that he is on trial. I don't know where we are. It is somewhere different. Another time and place.
You have been found guilty and are sentenced to death. I see my chance for escape and take it. We rush out the doors and disappear into the crowds of people.
You run to a friend's house and tell her you need provisions. She is the kind of person who can get you things.
Her brother is staying with her. I don't trust him. We exchange a few words. He doesn't like us very much. I wish he didn't know me. He is just the kind of person to turn you in for a reward. I don't think he knows we are on the run—that I have been found guilty of a crime.
She leaves to collect what you need. We begin exploring her house, looking for places to hide and ways to escape. Her bother leaves. I don't trust him.

We are standing by a door at the back of the house, in the basement. I see three guards running towards us with weapons in their hand. Her brother has betrayed us. They offered him a reward.
We run up the stairs and through the house. The girl is back and she runs with us. We burst out the front door and into a garden of flowers as tall as he is high. This is a good place to lose guards, but it's very hard to move—like dredging through sludgy clay.

I wish we had more time to create distance between them and us. In my minds eye I can see her brother holding the basement door closed so they can't get through. I don't know why he is doing this. He is helping us after betraying us. This will give us the time we need. They kill him.

We are carried away to the great stone building. I don't know why, but we often find ourselves here. It is a place of learning, but whenever we arrive, there is no one around.
You wander the halls and look into the rooms. *Abandoned.* You can see books piled high.
I know this place is haunted. I have been downstairs. I have been up in the attic that stretches beyond the physical dimensions of the building.
There is more to this place than appears. There is more to the city it belongs in. I have explored. I don't think this place exists in the waking world. I would be surprised if we discovered it. We only visit here in dreams. I come here when I am sleeping. I know areas of this city well.

NAVIGATOR

SPIRIT GUIDE

I had lunch with the medium today. To be honest, I don't really understand anything about what he does.
"It's real easy. Anyone can do it," he says, which comes as a shock to me. I mean, I thought seeing dead people was a talent you are born with.

I have come to accept the limitation of the human suit. There is going to be a lot we don't understand. Imagining that my logic will solve the riddles won't achieve anything but keep me distracted; wrapped up in my ego.
I know many people who have died. Their presence seems to stick around for a few weeks, and then they move on. I don't know how it all works, but this is how it seems.

Every good thing can end without a moments notice. I have seen it happen. Sometimes there aren't even warning signs, but there *is* something; something you can feel. In moments like this, we can discard how we feel in favour of what we want to believe. I call this intentional delusion.
We don't choose our beliefs; they are formed by our experiences.

It is a curious idea—death, and what happens after we depart.
When someone dies prematurely from suicide or an accident, I wonder if they are the ones to hang around the longest, searching for an answer to help them make sense of their experience.
I wonder if their essence attaches itself to material things like rooms or wood or chairs, the way memories attach themselves to tissue.

I suppose we all haunt one another, and maybe this is the problem. We were never meant to haunt one another, only enjoy one another and the human suit experience without attachment.
I don't know. I don't really have any of the answers.

I have spent the past couple days painting. Painting and cleaning. For some reason, the idea of only doing one thing and doing it thoroughly completely eludes me.
When I paint, it is all about risk. I paint in layers. I am constantly adding layers to my paintings. If I paint something I really like, I risk losing that by adding another layer. Sometimes the added layer doesn't work as well as what I had, so it becomes a challenge to redeem the changes I made. I keep doing this until it feels complete.

I try to set boundaries. Often I feel like I am a step away from where I should be—as though my lessons are happening too soon or not soon enough so nothing ever seems just right. Nothing seems complete.
This is what I am waiting for; for the ease and calm. For the end of struggle. For everything that has happened to make sense.
What will I do if I discovered that what I cherish most, no longer has value to me? Would I react or respond?
What happens when the change in me no longer supports the life I built for myself? Will I try and redeem the situation or discard it?
I continue painting and cleaning. I wonder if cleaning is also just an exercise in layers and redemption.

"If you want to find out who they are, just ask."
The medium said this about spirit guides. He said the spirit guides are the ones that help him learn the language of the dead.
He said he paid $450.00 dollars to take a weekend course and it boiled down to that—asking. They did a guided meditation up a mountain trail that led to a cabin. Sitting on the front porch was their spirit guide. That was it.
I am painting and cleaning. Maybe I should have sat down in some kind of posture that reflected a calm mind, but I wasn't calm. I live my whole life in layers, constantly trying to redeem the last move. How is that calm? I feel like chaos.

"Ok, I am ready. I am ready to listen and do what you say. I want you to show yourself to me."
Those were the words I used—or something close enough to that, and then I just continued painting and cleaning.
At some point I drew the brush back from the painting. I felt it was complete. I stepped back and looked at what I had done. I had painted a face.
His face is veiled. I had painted a veil so you can't see the facial features. I did this without even knowing I was painting a face, almost like I was caught up in some kind of trance.
GOEL.
I write the name in thick letters at the bottom right corner. I guess this is his name—my spirit guide, I mean.

I am putting on my shoes. The laces are tied and I look up as I begin to stand. Someone is in the chair by the window. GOEL.
He disappears.
"I was just startled," I say, aloud. "Thanks for showing yourself to me. Please do it again, anytime."

WARRIOR

The Cave

Take a moment to look around you. Notice the ground beneath your feet. What does it feel like?
I am standing in a field. It is early morning. The sun has yet to make an appearance. GOEL is with me. He is always by my side. He jumps around me playfully. We are not in a big hurry. We take time to enjoy the stillness.
In front of me are large rocks, like discarded pieces of a great mountain. If a giant came along he could reassemble them like completing a puzzle.
The rocks form a natural border between land and the Northern Sea. We walk along a well worn path. Many people have made this journey before me. We are going to a sacred place.
A single tear escapes my left eye—my feminine, creative and emotional side.

We are among the rocks, now. They are scattered but they start small. I think about the great mountain that once existed here. The one that is broken.
The path winds between the rocks. I lose sight of it as the rocks become larger. It is a kind of labyrinth.
Along this path is a cave. There are many caves.
You will enter the one that is right for you.
In order to be yourself completely, it is necessary to adopt a few clichés. If we knew all the options available to us, it would be so overwhelming that we would be unable to make a decision. Sometimes it's better to just *believe* that you will enter the cave you are meant to.

You can't see the cave from the path. There is a large boulder standing in front of the entrance. You literally have to go behind this boulder to access the cave. If you didn't know it was like that, you would walk right by. I didn't know, but I could feel it, and when I saw the boulder, I knew I had arrived
GOEL stops. He will not be following me inside. I consider the world I am leaving behind. My slowly going mad sister. My complacent mother. My brother who has died. My father whom I hate. I am journeying away from them all. It makes me sad, but sometimes the only way to change is not to remain the same; or perhaps the memories of what is to come, sadden me.

Inside the cave, I notice symbols on the walls. There is barely enough natural light to make out the sacred geometry left here. My fingers touch the symbols, sinking into the grooves like lines on a face, absorbing their strength.
The further in I walk, the lower the ceiling drops. I am hunched over and eventually crawl through a tunnel on my hands and knees.
There is no more light. I am alone in the dark.

There is a difference between loneliness and being alone. If you haven't figured that out yet, you are about to.

ARrKANA

Before The Flood

I emerge from the cave and gaze over the valley below. I take a deep breath and exhale. I have known this day would come for a long time, and have spent my life preparing for this moment; preparing myself to respond not react.
They will be watching for my peace. They must see the ease in me. This is my gift. I accept it.
It has taken me a lifetime to learn this gift. To learn that it can work for me or against me. To separate dreams and desires and destiny. To silence the chatter of my ego so I can simply *listen.*

Below me—where the valley empties into the ocean, is our village. To my right are rolling hills and grassy fields and the great city beyond them. I can hear children playing nearby. Their delight carries well across this valley. I begin walking down the mountain towards the village.
The homes are constructed very simply. This choice has been intentional. We wanted to create a community for ourselves that embraced the power and stability of nature.

Today my physical body will die. I look down at my arms; the worn out skin carries the wrinkles of an old man. As my fingers curl and wrists bend, I see glimpses of a luminous body beneath the human suit. I am old enough to remember when I didn't need this body.
I see my reflection, suddenly. It catches me by surprise. My white beard matches the thinning hair on my balding head.
I have lived a lifetime in this body and it shows.

A little girl runs up to me and throws herself into my arms. Her name is Kyeris. She has long brown hair. She weaves the sides around to form a braid in the back.
Kyeris is my granddaughter.
We have all known this day was coming, but she is still afraid. I look up and see her father—my son. He looks at me sympathetically.
I sit down and with Kyeris in front of me I begin to speak.
This is my job—my gift, to bring comfort and peace.
"This is the time of transition. It is something you must not fear," I tell her. "This is not an end, it is a beginning. Your luminous body will reform."
"I know that," she tells me, "but I love you. I don't want to be without you; not even for a moment."
"We will find one another again," I respond, my eyes glassing over with tears.
"But we will not be the same. I want you the way you are."
"Kyeris, my child, it is this kind of attachment that will not serve you. It will eat you up from the inside. You must not fear the death of your physical body because that fear will carry into your transition. It will become a blueprint on your soul."

How do I even begin to tell her that she will lose all memories of this place and the people here; that she will forget me and her mother and father and all of this until she finds us again, and even then—*maybe* she will remember us? It all depends on where her heart is at the time.
What we have in this incarnation will never be exactly as it is now. It may be similar. It may be so entirely different that the memories from this life will be as clear as a dream she can't remember, just feel.
I look up into her father's eye. He is standing tall and proud. He wants to protect her but understands his limitations. Trying to hold onto her now would make it worse for both of them. The only thing to be done is release. *Let go. Reborn.*
It is the hardest thing we will ever do and the most necessary gift we can give ourselves and those we truly love.

The longer we occupy this human suit, the more conditioned we become to the false sense of security that accompanies familiarity and routine. We become attached to the defaults of experience. Unless we embrace

the act of letting go, we will be ruled by fears of losing what we already have, never able to grasp what we may gain.
The very reason we came here gets buried alive in a prison of our own making.

I notice her mother hard at work. She is always busy doing things, even when there is nothing to be done. Right now she should be more of a mother and less of a busy body.
She has a hard time remembering who she was. She has made this physical vessel her home and as a result carries much anxiety. She thinks too much about the things she can't change and it eats away at her.
She wants things to stay the same but it is not meant to be. Her anxiety influences the ones she cares about most. This is why we should not live with anxiety. We should not accept it as a part of the cost for being human.
Intention directs us in life, in our transition, and where we end up in both.

We are all trying the best we can to have an authentic human experience, moulded by the personality we have developed and have been conditioned to believe is authentic.
I think back to an earlier time—before the formation of this community, when I was the age my son is now. We are standing in council in the city. You are not afraid to express how you feel. It earns you a reputation. You attract many people to you. Others resent you. They resent you for being comfortable enough to speak your truth. When you do, they are confronted with their truth and—if they are not walking and speaking and walking their truth, they don't want to be reminded.
This is what we are. This is what we are intended to be—a reminder. A reflection. A mirror.
Wouldn't it be nice to feel the love you are so willing to give?

When we made the decision to leave the city and form our own community on the coast, his wife was reluctant. She was not eager to abandon the things she had grown accustom to. Progress was making this civilization great and would make it mythical.
She could not understand our reasons. It very near tore their marriage apart before it had a chance to begin.

She loved him. Maybe she thought she could change him. Often the ones we love end up being the ones we put the most effort into manipulating. We don't want to be lonely. We become accustomed to having them around. They become our routines.
Life is full of change. It's scary to think the ones we depend on the most for the stability we crave are changing as well. What if they change away from us?
So we resist the natural flow of things. We try to dig in our claws and fight for the things.
It is a challenge to walk in a constant state of confidence; that place where we know our truth and don't let external situations or people control how we feel.

She was pregnant with their first child; I think that is why she stayed. I often wonder if their marriage would have ended otherwise. Within a few months of establishing our community on the coast she had a miscarriage. She blamed my son for that. She blamed me. But really, I think she was not ready to be a mother. She was unhappy with the lifestyle change. A child would have meant birthing in resentment and committing to a life she wasn't happy about.
I believe in things like that—that mothers influence the lives they carry inside them. Their feelings and emotions of things are felt by that little life, and that life will make decisions it believes are the best way to serve the one it loves.
We are born with that much love to give. Sometimes we give it away all at once and the lesson of our existence is complete.

After the miscarriage, she left our community. She went back to the city for three years. I think she was trying to figure it out. She was trying to force my sons hand. But she was asking more of him than to choose between her and me. I have no doubt he could have done that easily. It wasn't about me. She was asking him to choose between her and the very essence of his being—the thing every cell in his body prompted him towards.
Eventually she realized he could not sacrifice his essence for an illusion of love. Love never calls you away from your truth, it leads you to a better understanding of it. Anything else is desperation and insecurity.

Perhaps everyone goes there—to that dark place. The challenge is to realize the strength needed to pull yourself out is within you. It already is. The answers we need are within us. They don't come from outside of us. If we start thinking they do, we give our power away.

She moved back to our community and a few years later gave birth to Kyeris. Why did she move back? Her reason would not be the same as the one I would suggest. She moved back because she was lonely. It's a poor reason for marriage, but a common one. The men in the city that she had met and been with during those three years, they would not care for her the way my son did. Theirs was simply a mutual agreement. No one wants to feel loneliness. Everyone has their own reasons for that, or so they tell themselves.
She has always held me accountable for life not turning out the way she planned.

Kyeris wipes the tears from her eyes. She gives me a big hug, and places her hand in mine. She looks deep into my eyes, as if reading my soul. *Reading my soul.*
"It's time to go," she tells me.
"It is, my princess," I reply.
We begin walking.
As we make our way down the dusty streets of our village, others fall in step behind us. Her father—my son, meets my gaze. He nods at me silently, knowing what this moment means. That life presents us with opportunities to respond or react, and what we do in these moments determines how we will proceed through this miraculous journey we are all on; a journey to understand love in its fullness.

As a community, we walk. The village behind us now, the ocean stretching out in front. The sand between our toes, our gesture of resignation for which we humbly submit.
If there is any doubt amongst us, it disappears quickly as the tidal wave appears on the horizon.
What a great honour it is to transition surrounded by these people. The energy around me is swirling like the symphony of emotion I feel. The most beautiful thing is the lack of fear amongst us. How can there be fear where perfect love exists?

In perfect love, we can face the most terrifying prospects and rejoice.

My heart goes out to those in the city. When destruction catches up to them—unsuspecting as they are, they will transition in fear and self doubt. It will be encoded upon their soul. They will carry that anger and desperation with them. It will manifest as loneliness and the struggle to prove themselves worthy of the love they feel denied.
What a terrible way to enter new life. It will take a long time to get back to where they are now. A whole series of pain awaits them, necessary to work through the trauma of what they leave this life clutching.

With a subtle squeeze to my hand, Kyeris brings me back to the present moment. I lift her into my arms and hold her close to me. Next to me is my son, standing firm—standing proud, for all of us who don't feel that way. This is his gift.
The wave is closer now. It's size, intimidating. It's force, humbling. I raise my chin to greet this challenge. I express my gratitude for the opportunities I have had in this life to love, especially when it has not been returned to me. I entered into this life with full reserves of love. With whatever remains, I freely offer this child in my arms that she would have the strength—a reservoir of calm, to know her truth and transition in peace.

THE ONE THEY CALL THE VISION

LIGHTBEARER

I watch him enter the cave. It is very dark and he is holding a torch. He is crouched over, the ceiling of the cave forcing a posture of humility. The cave is narrow. Shadows dance on the wall, revealing strange symbols that can only be seen by a light bearer.
When I look at him again, I recognize myself. I am the one holding the torch, carrying it to the other side. I am the light bearer.

Suddenly we are in darkness. For a moment—as my eyes adjust, I see galaxies surrounding me. Stars and planets and colors and forms I can't explain.
Then a bright light appears. It is the light from outside. I have come through the passage and am approaching the other side. As my body comes into view, I begin to break away from it. I am an observer and the body emerging from the cave is the Warrior.
He moves around the bolder where GOEL is waiting for us. We begin walking away from the cave, around the worn out path that winds between the crumbled pieces of a broken mountain.
We walk into the field that stretches out before us.

We are far enough from the great boulders that they appear as rocks on the horizon. A luminous body appears in front of us, like a ghost. It is ArKana. I look into the face of the Warrior, and then at GOEL.
They look into mine.

The journey is just beginning.

COMMUNION

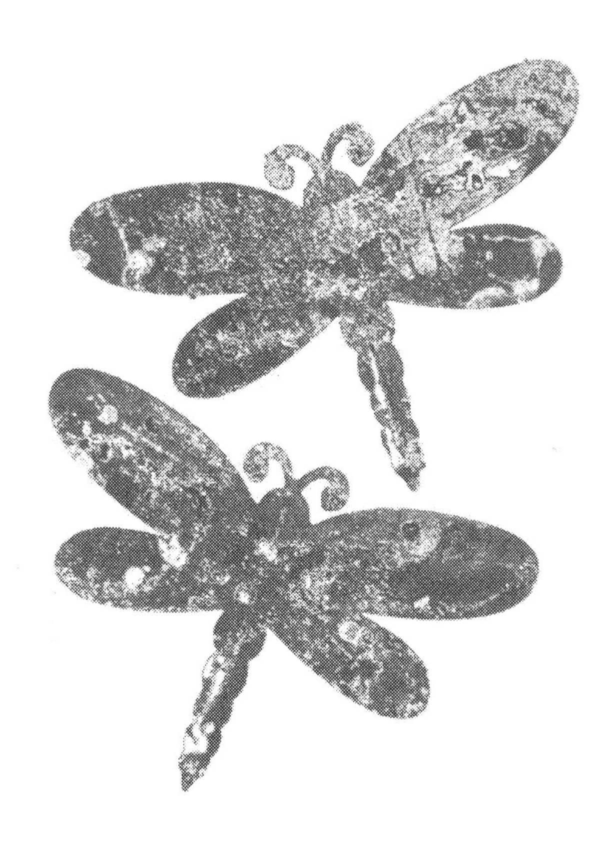

I wanted infinite existences with you. To forget you and meet you over and over again; to see you in different ways, to love you in different circumstances. That you would be mine and I would be yours forever. Only ever separated by temporary sleep, constantly in the process of waking up to you. That there would be no one else, only shadows of the plot dancing around us. Yes, I wanted infinite existences with you, but I couldn't be enough for even one.

David Brian Bootsveld
September 22nd, 1981—January 9th, 2012

THE ISLAND

My Only Home

This is how it begins.

You are standing waist deep in the ocean. An arm's length away is a raft, and on that raft is a box. Inside the box you place all the unwanted aspects of myself—the stresses and belief systems and things I can't change. You physically draw these things from my body and place them in the box.

I close the lid and turn your back to it. I jump into the crystal blue water, push the raft further out, and walk back to the white sandy beach with the polished lava rocks.

You lie down in the sand, in that spot where the ocean exhales. This place that is always wet and as soft as the universe between her legs.

The rhythm of the ocean adjusts to the rhythm of our breathing.

When I close my eyes, I am transported to other times—in other places, doing different things; leading different lives. I am in fields of sand. A large group of us are traveling. We are looking for something. *Symbols.* We are looking for symbols. Somewhere in this group is *my love.* The one I am looking for.

At night we put up tents in the fields of sand and the land of no water. She will be waiting for me there.

You awake with an awareness of time.

I open my eyes on the white sandy beach. The sun is in my eyes. I miss the one who is intended to be with me. I don't understand why she is not here. You are tired of being lonely.

You are lying on your back in that special spot. In my right ear, the sounds of the ocean. In your left, the jungle—and the particular silence of heat.

How long I have been lying here is hard to say. You feel completely at peace. Day turns into night and into day. The full moons and the sun seem to merge into one.

You feel as if the answers you seek are just out of reach. If only I could remember.
Memories—like shattered pieces of a mirror. We are not meant to do this alone. Another was with you.
There is nothing to fear with change, but letting go of things—even when they no longer serve us, can be scary.

The sun is high in the sky as you walk ankle deep in the ocean. I follow the length of the white sandy beach further than I ever have. Sand between my toes.
A dragonfly is above me. *My bothers.* Circling above me. He is nearly the length of my arm. The sound of his wings is soothing; a kind of white noise that drowns out my internal chatter.
I know nothing of this place or the sympathetic magic that occurs here. I look towards the jungle.
You are reluctant to admit it but this island feels familiar, like a dream I have forgotten and am just now remembering.
I cross from the sand to the jungle. The deeper in I walk, the more it changes. The trees change. I am no longer in a jungle but a forest.
You continue to follow a path, the one that has been laid out for us.

WARRIOR

We Both Go Down Together

I feel a million miles from home. I may as well be. I haven't even bothered to count the days since I left. Time is losing all relevance to me.
I ran. As fast and hard as I could. Ran from the fighting and my father. From my complacent mother and my slowly going mad sister. And from the memory of my brother.
I jumped at the opportunity to leave. I don't know what I would have done if I had stayed.
We have come to build this chapel and I am here for as long as it takes.

I've had a reoccurring dream since we left. I am back in the fields where we bury our enemies standing up. I am walking through the maze of hands stretched out of the ground like shrubs. Dried blood cakes their skin.
One of the arms reaches towards me. I become convinced the arm is my brother. I am on my knees clawing into the ground like an animal. He must still be alive. I must dig quickly before he breathes his last and his hand atrophies.
I am digging and digging. He is tall and his arm is so long.
When I reach the crown of his head, a violet light shines through the remaining dirt. It blinds my eyes. I keep digging. I dig behind his head so I can tilt it back and expose his nose.
I place my hands at his ears and roll his head back. A moment passes and I think it might be too late. Then I hear a great inhale of breath. I feel relief. I rest a hand on his cheek and the other blocks the sun from my eyes. I look into his face and see myself staring back.
Suddenly I am out of my body; an observer. I watch my physical self stumble backwards in shock, as other hands begin to move from within their graves standing up. One grabs at my ankle, and I fall to the ground.

Another clutches at my ear. I fight them off, stand and begin to run—but where is my brother? I know he is among the hands struggling for breath, digging their own way out of the ground. I must hurry or I will not escape. A hand scratches the length of my left calf. I draw my sword and slice through its forearm, and continue swinging wildly at all which obscure my escape.

SATORI

The Simplest Gesture Of Dignity

I am in a room with white walls and nothing but an old wooden chair in the middle. It faces two doors without handles. I don't feel trapped here. I sit down and wait.

It's hard to say how much time passes before the door on the right opens. I recognize the person who enters the room. They approach me. They stand in front of me without saying a word, then walk away—leaving through the door on the left. I feel like we have confronted something. *The separation between us.* This was someone I felt wronged me. They probably felt I wronged them. That's usually how it goes, both people have different versions of what reality is because each holds a unique perspective—their own.
Is this the reason I was brought here, to confront this person in silence? I don't know if you could call it forgiveness, but I feel better.
I am ready to move on when the door to my right opens. Again I recognize the person who enters as someone who has wronged me. Again they walk up to me silently and stand there without saying a word. The door on my right opens again. Another person I recognize walks in. Then another. They all take a turn standing in front of me silently and exit the door to my left.
The door to my right opens again. This time I see a line of people waiting to enter the room and stand in front of me. I recognize them all. Some of them are more significant to me than others but I realize the significance I placed on them is subjective. To those who felt I wronged them, it was *very* significant.

Sometimes it is easy to dismiss people and my behaviour towards them, especially when I don't understand their role. How do I determine who is significant to me? It comes down to whether or not I feel used; whether they contribute something to our relationship or just want something. Every relationship is based on some kind of a mutual agreement. Without proper balance, there is dysfunction.
Isn't it interesting that the simplest gesture of dignity is something I feel has to be *earned*.

There are so many people passing in front of me now—moving at such great speed, that it looks like one giant revolving door.
I am outside of my body observing the situation but feel I must return to it. I must be present for this process. I owe them—and myself, this much.
As I sit here, I feel the weight of misunderstandings relieved.

I become aware of a third door directly above me. It opens as my body lifts off the chair. I pass through it and find myself in darkness. I am suddenly very cold. I begin to see swirling colors and planets passing me. Stars and planets. I am moving through the tunnel to that place of birthing. I am moving faster and the colors blur and blend into a stream of light and sounds and memories.

I am standing in a garage. On the floor is a small child. I notice plastic tools on the ground next to him.
I have been here before. The boy turns around. He looks right at me. He is me.

"Why are you so worried?" he asks. "Remember what you already know and everything will be okay."
"Will it?" I ask doubtfully. He smiles.
"You already know it will. If you stop telling yourself stories of what life could be and start to appreciate what is in front of you, everything would be much easier for you. You can't figure this out. You only make it more complex by trying.
All of the tools you need to navigate your way through life are within you. There is nothing you need to understand that you don't already know. The consistency you are looking for is you.

You cannot blame others for failing to adopt the standards you set for yourself. You do this because you have created scenarios and outcomes in your head. Come back. Come back to reality."
"Which one?" I ask, laughing a little.
"It doesn't matter. The choices you make in one affect what happens in them all."

His mother calls from inside the house. *Our mother.* He stands and walks towards the door, then turns to face me one last time.
"Every choice counts."

I feel tempted to follow him inside but my vision gets blurry and I am in the darkness again.

NAVIGATOR

I Don't Know How Else To Love You

I don't remember whose idea it was. Dream experiments. We wanted to see if we could meet up while dreaming. Outside our physical bodies. On the astral plane.
We came up with different meeting places. One of them was a fountain in a courtyard, somewhere in Italy. Another was the island.
It didn't happen every night. Sometimes only one of us would remember. Other times we both did.

I was wandering through a snowstorm looking for her. The next morning she told me she was waiting in a cave for me. Outside was a snowstorm.
She told me that she had come to realize the cave was my consciousness—that she was hunkered down in my consciousness.
I wonder what she learned about me while in there. Did she know the significance of that cave in my journeys? I am certain I never shared anything about the field I was wandering through—the field with the bodies buried standing up.

This was how it began—I mean, *really* began, and things got pretty intense after that. We discovered quickly that in addition to dreaming together, we could leave our bodies and travel to one another. Often we would fall asleep this way. One of us would travel to the other and we would fall asleep together.
I remember the first time she came to me. I was lying in bed when suddenly there was a flash of white light. The whole room lit up. Another

time there was a loud crash. I climbed out of bed and searched all around for what had caused the sound but found nothing.
These were gestures; astral gestures. Things to introduce the change in energy.

Over the next few weeks our encounters grew more intense; more intense and more detailed. Swimming in the fountain. Traveling in Egypt. Sweating in the snow.
We are on the white sandy beach, her small body lying on top of mine in that place where the waters exhale. We look up at the stars too numerous to count, trying to find a way to connect them together and form some kind of picture. Imagining that if we could, then all of this will make sense; this thing we have—this ability. Our connection. I want to figure this out because there are things that don't make sense to me. Challenges. I seek answers to questions I don't understand. I want to know how she can live in different worlds at the same time. I want to know why she would want to.
I'm not sure she understands that the decisions she makes in this reality affect what happens in the alternates, as well. She is slowly going mad. We are not meant to live like this, with our feet in different places. Eventually we have to make a decision. The grass is greenest where you water it.
I don't know I am helping or hurting her by enabling this to continue.

All things come with a cost. The cost of filling your cup is emptying its previous contents. The cost of breathing is the exhale.
You pay a price to know more. Knowledge without application is fertile ground for hypocrisy.
Often we become so attached to what no longer serves us that we will continue with routine simply because it is predictable. Predictability provides us with the illusion of control in a world that offers us very little of it. This is how it works.
We aren't designed to control, just flow. Control is the dam in the universal river.
Maybe she feels like she has a lot to lose or maybe it's the uncertainty of gain which troubles her; not knowing if the next breath will be sufficient.

We travel to Egypt. It is one of our favourite places to go. She has koal around her eyes and long black hair. We are inside a tent, pillows covering the ground. We are tangled. We make love for hours, and I awake in the morning more exhausted than I was before sleeping.
In daylight, another reality takes over. A great chasm separates us for which there are nether trees big enough nor vines long to help us cross over. This doesn't stop me from trying. I don't know how else to love her. She is my princess. She awakens from her coma sleep only when the chatter of the world around her—a world which offers her a security she has grown to depend on, dies down. Or frustrates her. Then I become the attic door.

I spend a lot of time trying to be grateful for the beauty in front of me. It does me no good to dwell on things I can't change. I have already failed miserably, watching my self-preservation confuse my happiness with the source point of pain I manifest.
There is a belief system that suggests if you don't try and manipulate circumstance then you are indifferent, gutless, lacking confidence or a coward. I am not any of those things. Why would I want to try and control the flow of something that was never mine? Any form of manipulation would only cause me to judge myself and resent others.
Letting go is tough. It's like amputating an arm that never existed but you have allowed yourself to believe was essential.

I have spent most of my life believing that I was missing something that would make me feel complete. A conviction of purpose drove me to seek out answers and in the process I have realized something quite profound: as soon as I start believing that the answers I need originate from somewhere outside of myself, I begin descending into madness.
I believe in a plan. Some kind of cosmic master plan. I couldn't tell you what that is, or what my role is, but we are a part of it.

Underlying the success of every journey is the absence of receiving the things I desire. I believe we can get anything we want from this life, but there are guidelines we must follow. Our desires must originate from within. Expecting others to adapt to us will only result in blaming them for how we feel. Only you are responsible for your feelings. Why would I give that power away?

The only person you will ever change with intention is yourself. Change yourself, and others will change because they see change in you. Try and control others, you will only succeed in alienating people.
This is the power of influence.

Self preservation that is not anchored in the heart will always lead to sabotage, because it is based on logic.
The mind tries to come to terms with the navigation of the heart. Logic suggests everything that comes to us is ours and needs to be held onto. I don't agree. Logic doesn't understand emotion. It only understands survival.
Experience is multidimensional; a constant process of letting go like the duality of breathing. We need oxygen to breath but we must exhale. Trying to remain in control is a restrictive posture, like holding your breath. The release is equally important. We surrender our ability to control. We make a gesture towards the Divine. It is essential to the mechanics of breathing.
Everything in nature follows this pattern. The rhythmic inhale and exhale of the ocean, for instance.

Heart knowledge is the absolute confidence of a thing. There is no need to contemplate the decision, you just act because you trust what you already know.
When we listen with the heart instinctively, we begin remembering more of why we are here. What we are intended to learn. *Our purpose.*

The power of intention. The written word. These are two things I must learn more about. They possess the power of creation.

NOGWAL

Into The Deep End

Alone in the dark. It feels like I am floating in water yet I am not wet. I don't think I am dead. I don't think terms like that exist in this place. I am an observer inside some kind of body. Probably not a physical one. I look into the swirling colors because in them I will see something. Some vision. Some clue.

Two years of swimming lessons taught me nothing. I spent most of the following summer with my knees bent, walking around the shallow pool flailing my arms.
One day someone told me they knew I couldn't swim; they knew I was walking around the pool with my knees bent. I felt humiliated. That was the day I taught myself to swim. I walked over to the adult pool and jumped in. I landed in the water, turned around and pulled myself out. Then I walked a few steps deeper and jumped in again. I did this up the length of the pool then climbed onto the diving board and jumped into the deep end.
That's how I learned how to swim. That's how to get things done.

I hated sports. Actually, I hated the competition. I was a sensitive little boy who liked to draw and listen to his dads Johnny Cash records. I didn't really have friends and totally lived inside my head. Then high school came and everything changed. I went to a new school where no one knew me. They didn't have a story of me they told themselves.

I ran for class president as a way of earning some position within an already established social hierarchy. I designed pamphlets to hand out. A list. Why I Don't Want To Be Your Friend.

I can't remember them all but they were things like: *You will only disappoint me and I will come to regret having invested the effort in you.*

Those ten reasons became my identity for the next decade, an identity based entirely on the theory that the best way to attract people was to act completely indifferent to them.

There is some truth to this—enough truth that I became class president that year. People are attracted to what seems elusive to them, but it comes with a catch. Once people accept the mystery, they are content to keep you that way, and when I need people around me, no one is interested or available. I think it scares them because suddenly they discover I have emotions.

I have become the attic door—the kind others are afraid to open; content enough to wait until they need an escape.

THE ISLAND

Do You Like Where We're Headed

Ahead of you is a wooden bridge. The bridge crosses a stream.
My bothers is above me. *Who is guiding who?* Soon I will remember everything. I will fall into her eyes.
We cross the bridge and the path curves.
There is a house just off the path, tucked amidst the trees. It has no roof and strange symbols on the walls. *The symbols we were looking for in the fields of sand and land of no water.*
As you continue on the path I notice more houses without roofs. This all seems familiar. I quicken my pace, knowing something greater awaits me to account for the favour that has been given to me.

The forest empties into a village. I can hear voices and smell smells. The creaking wheels of a cart rolling; children playing.
These memories are ghosts. The village is deserted. I am alone. I don't remember what happened to everyone, but somehow I *know*. I feel the memories. They fill me with an awkward mix of anxiety and curiosity.
I continue to walk through the abandon village and eventually come upon a great stone building. It seems to be a place of worship or learning.
It is vacant of furnishings. I notice an elevated area in the middle of the room and walk towards it. At the center is a platform and some kind of navigational instrument. When I place my hand on it, time accelerates.
I don't know how long I have been here. I watch the sun shine down in the day; I see the full moons illuminate the night.

NOGWAL

This Is Going To Be Fun

Why haven't I thought of this before? Maybe all I need to do is open my eyes. I want to open my eyes.
Instantly I see colors around me. Stars and planets and the shape of things I don't understand. I am moving through space.

"Where do you want to go?" a voice asks.
I am looking at the earth. I begin to descend upon the planet.
I am standing on the sidewalk of a major city. People are passing on either side of me and the sounds of traffic fill the streets. I know this place well. I tilt my head slightly and all the people are gone. The traffic has disappeared. I tilt back and they return. *Interesting.*
I start walking, experiencing the different realities with the movement of my head.

I come across a little girl. She is only there when everyone else has disappeared. I tilt my head back just to make sure. I don't see her in the reality of people and traffic, but I do notice that up ahead, traffic has come to a halt. There has been an accident. Now I understand. I tilt my head and return to the deserted city. I am unsure if she can see me. Then she looks up and speaks.
"Where has everyone gone?" she asks. "I can't find anyone. Do you know where they are?"
I look into her watery eyes. She doesn't even realize that she is dead. *She died in the accident.*
I crouch down in front of her.
"You know the kind of love you have for your mommy," I start.
She nods, and places her hand in mine.

"That love—even a greater love, is waiting for you. The gift of everlasting love."

She looks into my eyes, sobbing, and I know she understands. She gives me a hug. It reminds me of something. A memory I have forgotten. *My granddaughter.*

Instantly she is gone.

I shoot into the air and travel far from the city.

I descend into a railway yard. There is an old man walking along the tracks. When he sees me drop out of the sky, he stops. His mouth is hanging open. He can't believe what he has just seen. I walk over to him.

"That's impossible," he starts. "How did you do that?"

"You're right," I reply. "It is impossible. You're dead."

He disappears.

This is going to be fun.

A YOUNG PRINCE IN DISQUISE

Do You Reach Out For My Arm

I am riding a horse. We travel across fields of ice and snow and sand. Through forest and jungle. Over hills and valleys and oceans.
Beside me is GOEL. He keeps pace, effortlessly. He never seems to tire. He travels with me. He always has.
We have been on this journey for such a long time. A journey towards freedom.

I have a funny relationship with pain. Without it I wouldn't know a thing. Pain lets me know when to pay attention. It manifests when I am not listening to what I know is true. *My personal truth.* But pain also lies.
There comes a point when we realize that the world is different than our own experience; when blaming others for our pain no longer makes sense, because pain originates from within. It's something we control. Even if I give that power away, pain remains a result of what I am doing to myself.
The experience of pain is personal.

Truth is the mirror. It will never reveal what to do, only what is. It's up to me to make the observation. Change begins with the acknowledgement of truth; the awareness of a thing.
The point isn't to judge ourselves just discover ourselves.

There is a shortage of listeners in this world because everyone has a desire to be heard so badly.
I have a theory that we become who we are seeking. If you are a listener, it's because you want to be listened to. If you are a nurturer, it's because

you want others to nurture you. If you offer love, it's because you desire love.
When others fail to recognize my needs, I resent them—even if I have perpetuated the story that keeps them from noticing. When others don't treat me the way I expect—in a way that supports the story you tell myself, I feel dehumanized; not valued.
You often look outside yourself for things I already possess.

All the tools I need to handle the challenges of this his life have been placed inside me. The situations that overwhelm you are the ones I create through stories I tell myself, based on past experiences and the assumption that history will repeat itself.

We are a species that craves community. Within community, you desire to fulfill a role for which we will be appreciated and feel valued.
Our personality reflects how we intend to attract the community we are seeking. Our ego is like a shield, in the event I am rejected.
I built a strategy for coping with rejection. This strategy became the shackles to a past that I was unable to heal. Without healing the wounds of the past, it is impossible to move forwards; to reach my destination.
Hopelessness is comforting if you are more afraid of change than you are of staying the same.

Words aren't nearly as powerful as our ability not to speak. Silence is often the most powerful tool available to us.
I find it way too easy to resent people who want to be heard if they refuse to listen back.
It doesn't take long for people to become dependent on a listener, and it doesn't take long for a listener to become intoxicated with being needed, especially when that is what I seek most.

I have been on this journey for so long that I don't even remember when it began.
From the moment we enter into this world we begin seeking love and approval—measuring what we receive by what we are willing to give. It becomes our standard.
Perhaps this is not such a good ideal. I am unsure anyone is capable of the standards I set for myself. They have their own standards based on

experiences and belief systems that are different than mine. Who am I to question those? Or tell them when they should abandon their armour.

The only way to truly love someone is to allow them to make their own decisions. To trust whatever force is guiding me on this journey is also guiding hers.
Be grateful for every breath. It is a gift. And then exhale.

CONQUERER

Does It Make Sense In Your Eyes

Some things are inevitable. I never considered myself a fatalist but since I have been on this black rock castle—towering out of the sea in rebellion, I have had a lot of time to think.
Every night I look across Oceans Gate towards the hill where *my love* breathed her last. Every night I relive those final moments before hope died. Hope for restoring Priveden. Hope that everlasting love was greater than mortality.
The more I witness this scenario replay itself, the more I torment myself, imagining that I could have changed things.
Even worse, I died knowing I was not the person I thought I was.

I have considered throwing myself into the violent waters but it feels like a futile gesture. I am already dead. I must be here for a reason. I may as well wait and see what it is.
My only company is a large dragonfly. *My bothers.* He circles above me, humming. His wings sound like battle drums.

Sometimes when I tilt my head, I see things in the sky. I can't make out their shape, but they are there—hiding behind clouds and the heat that burns my skin.
I think my eyes are adjusting to this new reality because I have begun to see boats in the violent waters. Boats that were always there. Somehow I know this.

Within this black rock prison, I have discovered caverns and holes large enough to burrow into. I am carving out a home for myself. It is incredible what one can do with intention.
I imagine being here with *my love*. Reunited in death. A cosmic love story that endures.
I must find or create hope. What else am I to do? Hope is momentum. Survival depends on it.
I must continue to believe in the love I have experienced. I must continue to believe that it exists without allowing my past to be the standard for this present reality. History is not bound to repeat itself. I believe I can change things.

This is a time for reflection. Of learning to be silent and appreciate the sympathetic magic that brought me to this place. It brought me here for a reason. I am sure to discover this.
I must keep hope alive, even if hope remains hidden behind the light that gets in my eyes.

WARRIOR

Blood In The Snow

I have another dream. This one isn't like the reoccurring one, it's more like a memory.
It happens in the winter when there is snow on the ground. I am sitting on a stone wall watching *my love* below.
She is aware I am watching and looks up at me. We fall into one another's eyes.

This thing we have—that we have discovered, is incredible. We travel together. We move through the timestreams, acting out different roles in each lifetime. Always searching for the other. Searching even if we don't know we are searching. And when we find one another, we begin remembering. We remember what we already know. All the memories we have collected together. All the pain and sorrows and happiness and ecstasy.
There is always a challenge. Some new thing we must learn. The role we play reveals the challenge, and what we do once we have identified the challenge is how we integrate the lesson.

She is in the snow and we exchange seductive glances. She calls to me with her eyes. I leap off the snow and move towards her.
This moment has been brewing for a long time. Like a pot with hot water in it. And when moments like these come, all you can hope for is that self preservation works for you not against you.

The humming gets louder. Their shadows dance in the snow as they circle above us. We fall into the snow; bodies becoming tangled. Sweating in the snow that doesn't even feel cold against our naked skin.

It is evening and I am in my father's chamber. He is drunk and making bad decisions. I walk out of the room. For a moment I think of asking GOEL to kill him.
He calls for mother. As we pass, her eyes betray what she lacks the courage to speak.
My sister runs over to me and throws herself in my arms.
"What has happened?" she asks.
"Let us go outside. There are full moons tonight."

We pass beyond the walls that surround our home. The moonlight bathes the fields, reflecting off the fresh snow. The smell of the Northern Sea fills the air with a scent of violence and mourning.
I lay down in the snow, the furs on my back like a blanket beneath me. *My love* lies down on my body. Her head on my chest.
We don't speak because we speak without words. This is what we do. This is what we have always done.

As children, my mother would often sit with her at night because she had the worst time sleeping. When this began to irritate my father the task was passed onto me. One night as I lie next to her, she rolled on top of me and fell asleep with such ease it was as though she had been drugged. That night I dreamt of an island with strange trees and crystal blue water.
I woke up in the morning feeling like all the tension inside of me had been relieved; as though roots stretching from my body had been given a chance to relax.

Over the years, I watched over her as brothers do. She continued to fall asleep on my chest and one night I dreamed she was with me on the island.
The next morning she told me that she dreamed we were on an island with strange trees and crystal blue water. And the dragonflies—she saw the dragonflies! *Our bothers.* One flies above her and the other above me. They are like homing signals, guiding us back to one another.

My brother cautioned us to keep all of this from our parents. He said they would not understand this kind of sympathetic magic, so we kept it secret.

When I was at war she became immobilized, leaving our mother to do all the household chores.
Our dreams became more intense. It wasn't just the island and the Nogwal, but a black rock castle, a city of stone and health and separation, and fields of sand—where we are married. We have a daughter. She is a *God of the New World.*
These are the memories I wake up to. As real as what I do in waking life. How do you suppose I manage this?
Is history reoccurring or running side by side? Is my freewill an illusion or do my choices matter? And do they have the power to change things?

We returned from war without my brother. We lost him in battle. From that point on, things began to change. Father began drinking and mother became subservient.

I don't know how much time passes. It is becoming increasingly irrelevant to me.
I want to figure this out. There is so much we are remembering. What I don't understand are the challenges.
Normal has become subjective. Self preservation outweighs it. I refuse to allow the standards of others to determine how I live my life and what I will do with the opportunities—the options, available to me.

We have left the fields. We are sitting on the great stone wall that overlooks the Northern Sea. Moonlight illuminates the raging waters below us.
"Father has decided it is time for you to marry," I reveal.

Our father is a selfish man, and a jealous one. He is jealous for power. With the death of my brother, he was forced to recognize that he is not in control.

How quickly everything can change. One moment the entire world seems yours for the taking and then next—you are the one being taken.
Every story he told himself—of how together with my brother they would make our family name powerful, disappeared in a moment. He sunk into a violent kind of self loathing which he took out on anyone around him.

"Am I merely a pawn to him? Surely he desires only to hurt you by this."
"Nothing can ever come between us," I reply, avoiding her insinuation which I know is true, "not even this."

With my brother gone, the survival of the family rests on me. It is not a burden I desired, nor do I want. Marrying off *my love* was mother's suggestion, no doubt. She has begun to suspect that our sibling bond has grown into an affection that threatens the strength and survival of the family name.

"If we hang on to this," I continue, "we could lose everything. I don't know what is right or wrong. All I know is there is a lesson we are intended to learn and the choices we make will determine where we end up next—and how difficult it will be to remember and find each other in the next transition."
"How much more separation must we endure? Why can't we be together now?" my love asks.
"We will find one another again," I respond. "Nothing can separate a love like this."
"But we will not be the same. I want you the way you are. I don't want to be without you, not even for a moment."

We sit on the wall in silence. The refection of the moonlight on the water. Her body leans into mine. My left arm—the emotional one, curls around her small body. The wind is gently blowing through her wild mane of hair.
How much time passes, I can't say. It has lost all relevance to me.

"Have we no other options?" she finally speaks, looking up into my eyes. Her eyes—*the gift of everlasting love.* How I long for her. This love we share is my completeness. *I could die right now and be content.*
"I could die right now and be content," she echoes back to me. "I just want to sail away from it all."
"Hush, *my love.* I don't want you to disappear. Now watch the moons. It will be over quickly. I promise."

She lays her head on my chest. Inside my boot is a dagger. I reach for it with my logical arm. She is singing a charming kind of lullaby, a sacrifice offered up for what I am about to do. Her voice haunts me already.
I kiss her softly and with a final gesture of resignation, allow my fingers to brush across her cheek, tracing the lines and feeling her warmth a final time.

The blade slices mercilessly across her throat. I plunge the dagger into my heart. Our bodies slump forward and plunge into the raging Northern Sea.

NAVIGATOR

He Opens His Eyes And Falls In Love At First Sight

I leave my physical body and travel to her room. She tells me she has been waiting for me. I settle my body next to hers. We are made for this. This is what we do.

"I dreamed of you again," I tell her. She is stroking my hair.
"Tell me."
"You were teaching others. Your parents didn't understand. One of the greatest challenges of being a parent, I think, must be learning from your children."
"What did they learn from me?"
"That all you needed was for someone to believe in you and then you believed in yourself."
She doesn't say anything in response. We fall asleep tangled in one another.

I open my eyes and find myself on a sidewalk early in the morning. I feel compelled to walk down the middle of the road. A car is headed straight for me. It does not have a chance to slow down. It passes right through me.
In that instant, all traffic and people disappear. I begin to hear music, like a soundtrack.
I hear *my love*. You aren't anywhere I can see. You tell me I am sleeping and you have some things to show me.

I am walking down the middle of the street and you tell me to open my eyes—not my physical eyes but my other eyes.

"I'm not really sure how to do that," I respond and you tell me you will help me.
"You must learn to breathe," you continue "There is a cylinder that runs through your body. Fill this cylinder with breath."
I look down at my body and I can see this through my clothes and skin and bones. It's like a tube running through me.
Suddenly—on my right, I see snow materialize on the ground. We are making love in the snow. My hair is longer. You look exactly the same. I have seen this before. I have *lived* it.

As I continue walking, more images appear as the ones I pass fade away. It's like I am watching silent movies and constantly find myself in the lead role.
To my left is the jungle and we are running through it, giant dragonflies above us. We are on a boat in the early morning hours. You hold a baby in your arms. We are in Egypt. We are standing in the doorway by which faeries enter our world. We are floating through the cosmos watching planets being born and stars explode.
To my right is a great wall, overlooking the ocean, bathed in the light of twin moons.
Every scene is familiar to me and I find myself amazed at what I am observing.

"Why are you showing me all these things?" I ask.
"So you understand. Our higher selves made an agreement long before either of us began this journey. We are learning how to love. We are teaching one another. All the choices we make affect every choice we've made. Do you understand?"

THE ISLAND

All Our Defences Are Down

It is night. You leave the great stone building. You pass a tower and move beyond the village without roofs to where a fire burns. Around it are stones and logs for sitting. I stare into the flames and wonder who started this fire and where they are now.
I become aware of someone watching me from inside the flames. They aren't inside the flames, they are on the other side of the fire looking through.
It is a little boy or girl of Asian or African descent. They don't say a word. Perhaps they are unable to speak or simply don't need to. It's not like I am speaking. We are speaking without words.

As the flames dance around like faeries, I am drawn into their eyes. I am pulled in and I start falling. Falling off the wall and into the raging Northern Sea. Falling through the tunnel with the swirling colors. Falling through the pink clouds towards the ocean; into the water and sinking with momentum. I pass through the ocean floor and move effortlessly through layers of sand and clay and gravel and rocks. I enter a cavern and my body slowly lowers to the floor.
Hovering above is *my bothers*. His hum alerts me that *my love* is near. She is wandering somewhere in the dark. I have come to take her away from this prison of her own making. I call out to her and she answers me.
I see *her bothers* before I see her.
She emerges from the dark. She walks over to me, dressed in rags. I hold out my hands to her. *My love. Princess of the Timestreams. Seamstress of my destiny.*
She places her hands in mine.

"You don't have to stay here," I begin. "You only have to be willing to let this place go and the things that no longer serve you. You're higher self is waiting for you. I have seen her. I see her all the time. If you are ready to leave, we can go now."

She stands behind me and wraps her arms around my chest—one hand on my heart, the other below my naval. Violet light pours out of our chakras and covers us. We begin to rise into the air and shoot up at great speed. Through the ceiling of this cavern. Through the rocks and gravel and clay and sand. Through the ocean floor and amidst the tide that moves the lava rocks. We emerge from the depths and ascend like sparks into the heavens, by reflection of the twin moons. We leave the planet's atmosphere and enter space where the colors swirl and the planets dance like flames.

I am on my knees. The child stands in front of me. I am startled when they speak, only because I don't expect it.
"I am everything you want."

They turn and walk away. I stand and follow.

True mystics are pursuing the experience of the Divine. They aren't interested in theories and words because no amount of either makes a thing real, they only form belief systems which prevent us from remembering the truth we already know.
Humans are the only species designed in the image of divinity. We are creational. This is our power.
My only theology is that I am pursuing truth.
Our voice moves like a wave. With it, we live in harmony or discord.

THE PAIN STATION

ENCHANTED

I am sitting in the backseat of a car. You look out the window and it's dark outside. We got lost off the freeway. She is on the phone getting directions.
We are back on track, moving through the deadened streets to an unrecognizable house in a cul-de-sac.

The Pain Station is not so much a secret as it is legend. You find yourself rolling up on the place wondering how this is happening to you. You can't strategize these moments. They just happen and it's on us to seize them or let them slide by.
Today I set a precedent for the rest of my life. I don't want to live in a prison of my own making—a casket shaped reality, I want to take all I can get.
People who are truly happy, they seize moments as if every passing one can alter their life. They live without the absolutes that prevent others from moving forward. Their self preservation works *with* them.

She is one of the first people I meet who will not allow her logic to manifest as inhibition. She is logical as well as creative—a rare breed. It must be very hard for her, I decide, and tell her this. She laughs. We become inseparable.
She is different. I am enchanted.

SATORI

At Least We Both Have Been Relieved

We are in the white room with three doors. She is sitting in the wooden chair. I am kneeling in front of her.
"Sing me the lullaby," I ask.

I am on the chair, now, and she is on her knees in front of me.
"Receive your grace," I whisper.

Why should I ever be asked to let go of *my love*?

THE PILOT

Don't Let Me Fade Away

So you and me are flying through this bright collared tunnel—a psychedelic tunnel, and we are moving so fast. We are flying up to the astral plane. Our bodies have just left their human suits and together we are returning to our home in the stars.

While we travel I see visions of our lives through time. I see us in Egypt in the pillow tent. I see us exploring the island and laying in that special spot in the sand where the ocean exhales. I see so many different places we are together. I see us sitting on the wall—my body leaning into yours. I can't even sit up. I am so dizzy because my spirit hasn't fully connected with my body because it is with you, in another place.

We arrive at the Nogwal, in our own little bubble, waiting to be reborn again. Entwined in the cosmos—the stars, our background. It is magnificent.

We aren't meant to go through this life alone. It takes a different kind of strength—a different kind of love, to embrace people when we are hurting. We hurt because people don't act the way we would; the way we want them to.

As we work our way towards being whole, our expectations of others sabotage us. We judge ourselves based on our intentions and others by what they do. This is why we seek mercy for ourselves and justice for others.

Our journeys through the timestreams continue to show me how much I neglect to embrace this amazing experience of life. Life with you. Again.

I think our higher selves laugh at our naivety and comfort us when we cry.

I want to experience what makes you laugh. I want to know your smile and fall into your eyes and discover your soul. I want to recognize your touch and be drawn into your magnetic pull. I want to read together in bed and talk of finding one another again and again in all the lifetimes we share; to remember who we are and give in to the enchantment of this great spell.
Your energy illuminates my spirit. My desire to hold you is overwhelming. Every cell in my body calls out for you. I stare wide eyed into your soul with gratitude.

Close your tired eyes and fall asleep in my embrace. Our spirits know where to go. They know to be together. In the lives we've shared and the lives to come. On every plane and dimension of existence. You are everywhere, and everywhere you are I will be.

The physical world is too careless with memories. Don't let them fade away. Don't let *me* fade away.

Under A Blanket Of Peace

I love the smell of rain. It makes me think of rebirth and new beginnings. Last night we rode through a storm. The sky lit up in flashes. Thunder rolled like drums. Rain fell violently, and with force.
We found shelter in a cave and I stayed awake as long as I could, enjoying the fact that I was not the only one mourning tonight.

I'll be honest with you, sometimes I feel like I don't want to continue this journey. Sometimes I want to turn around and go back home; only I am not sure I know where home is anymore.

You are thinking that I should be more positive, but that doesn't mean much coming from you. It sounds like a cliché because you don't have anything intelligent to say. And when people don't know what to say, they settle for a lot of things they don't mean.
All you see are the moments of my life like a collection of stars, and that looks pretty good to you. But if you were me, you would know that those stars form no constellation. All I have is a collection of moments with no way to weave them together. No consistency.
What makes you think I would want to be a support to anyone without becoming emotionally involved? I would just feel used and resent myself for the lack of dignity and self respect I was willing to give myself.

It has been raining lightly all morning. I don't mind it as much as my horse does. Actually, I enjoy it. It is comforting. I don't feel so lonely. Despite how I torment myself throughout the day, at night—when we sleep, I know better.

THE ONE THEY CALL THE VISION

Clowns In Coffins

I watch myself. I am six years old, standing in the lobby of a funeral home. Through the doors is a dead man. My parents said he was a family friend and that is why we are here. I remember him only as a big fat man who dressed as a clown on the weekend and stood in the mall handing out balloons to children.
He died almost a week ago.

I haven't thought about death too much.
"It's when the spirit leaves the body," I tell my mother, "and goes to heaven to eat the bread of life with Jesus."[1]
To be honest, I don't even know what the that means, but I heard the line in a movie and it sounded like a sad and mournful thing. The kind of thing you should say when someone dies.
My mom seemed to approve so I will take every opportunity to say this today.

The big doors open and I walk into the room. The seats are arranged in front of the dead man. He is in a long box with his picture on top.
We sit down and I watch people cry.
I am crying now—caught up in the frenzy. It will probably make people feel better if they see me this way.

A man stands behind the box at the front of the room. The box with the lid open. He looks depressed and starts speaking.
"We're all going to die. It could be in twenty years. It could be tonight."
He pauses for dramatic effect.

---

[1] The Stand, Stephen King

"At times like these, we've been taught to lie. We go through so much trouble to avoid the unavoidable and prolong the pain of being alive."[2]

When he stops speaking, there is complete silence. I notice a red hummingbirg flying over the box at the front of the room. The sound of wings flapping in the air.

People get out of their seats and walk forward. They are waiting in line to look at the dead man. I get out of my seat. I want to see what they see.

On my journeys through the timestreams, I have seen myself die many times. That would be worrisome if I believed that all time is measured the same way, but it's not. The movement of time is measured a lot differently.
By the time a dog turns one, their body has reached the development of a human teenager. Their second year is about another ten of our years. Every human year thereafter, they continue to age another five to eight in comparison to us—depending on their size and breed.
Imagine if you could take the lifespan of a dog and stretch it out to match the length of your own. Time would be moving so slowly that every passing moment of that dog's life would seem to drag on mercilessly, like going to see a movie and being given a stack of frame by frame photographs to go through.

Some things are inevitable, but options always exist. They exist between the frames. This is when we can change things.
Our choice to react or respond to the inevitable determines the amount of suffering we bring on ourselves.
Make sense? That's okay if it doesn't. I am six years old, what do you expect?

2 Priests and Paramedics, Pedro The Lion

It's my turn to look in the box now. I stand on my toes and can barely see over the edge. He's wearing that stupid red nose and his face is painted white with big purple cheeks.

I'm not sure it really happened that way, but that's how I remember it.

WARRIOR

Fields Of Snow And Ice

I am walking through a raging snowstorm. I can almost see rocks in the distance. The place where a mountain once stood.
Is this where I am supposed to be?
Suddenly I am carried away. Colors are swirling. I am moving through the psychedelic tunnel.

Time has accelerated or reversed. I am walking through a field of ice and snow. The storm is over. The sun is shining. Underneath me, frozen bodies reach out for their lost manhood, now broken and carried off by wild beasts.
I hear them wailing.

There is a place where the ground slopes down. A great structure once stood here. *A great stone structure.* All that remains are the guts.
GOEL guides me here. He is my guide. I know this. He travels with me. They all work together but function differently-GOEL, *my bothers*, and the red hummingbird. And someone else. *Something else.*
I am remembering so many things but not enough to feel in control. Maybe that's the point. Maybe the real learning begins when I stop trying to participate and just let it happen.

An iced over staircase is carved into the ground. I climb down.

CONQUERER

I Will Endeavour To Be Home

We have constructed a home for ourselves within the black rock castle and made ourselves a fortress.
To be honest, I don't remember when she appeared but hell has been replaced with a kind of paradise.
Sometimes I question if she is real. If any of this is real, but I don't question too much. Perhaps because I don't want to know the answers. I can come to terms with slowly going mad, now that *my love* is here with me.

We have a home. Our room is round. We can look out and see the violent waters of Oceans Gate, and the village on the mainland.
Looming behind Sinister is the hill where *my love* breathed her last breath. Sometimes late at night, I sit on cliffs under the light of full moons. Since *my love* has come to me, the orbs have ceased ascending nightly. Slowly that reality is fading, like the details in my memory of the life we once lived. Maybe this is for the best. There is a kind of grace in forgetting.
My love seems to have no memory of that life at all, and I haven't reminded her. Whatever sympathetic magic that is at work here, I must trust it. I don't put a lot of effort into trying to understand things I am unable to. And I don't think it is for me to question. I am content to accept an eternity with *my love* even if eternity is spent on this black rock tower, spit out of the sea in rebellion.

My love comes to me. I am high above our home watching the moon's reflection dance on the water like flames of fire. She lies on my chest. There are too many stars to number but it doesn't stop us from trying. We name them all. We name them after the *Gods of the New World.* We imagine them to be our children, born with a conviction of purpose and the resolve to follow through. Redeeming the lives we lost to name them here tonight.

NOGWAL

Tell Me Now And Tell Me This

I am moving quickly through a tunnel of black and spiralled colors. My vision begins to adjust as my form slows. I am floating, watching planets circle suns.
There are clouds in space. Colored clouds. They spin and twist around one another like complex strands of DNA.
I stare into them and see visions of lifetimes I have lived or will live. My eyes grow heavy with longing for all that I am missing.

With money I saved, I buy an angel for the Christmas tree. My plan is to sneak downstairs and place it while everyone is sleeping, as a surprise.

On Christmas morning I join the rest of the family around the tree. I am more excited to see their reaction to my angel then I am to receive presents.
I keep waiting for them to notice. No one has said a thing. Finally I can't take it anymore. I ask where the angel came from. My father casually says something like, "you put it there," and continues his role as master of ceremonies.
That's it. It's like no one even cares that I made the effort.

When I was in grade four I joined the school band. I choose the alto saxophone. After months of investment, I still couldn't play the thing.

There was a recital in the school auditorium one evening. Parents and guests came. I wasn't actually nervous because I had a strategy—puff out my cheeks and move my fingers up and down the horn.
When the recital was over I made my way into the audience to find my parents. Someone—I don't remember who, congratulated me on my solo. They had trouble hearing it but could tell I was playing a solo because my fingers were moving differently than the other alto saxophone players.

I just want things to be easy. I want the lessons to stop long enough that I can depend on something—*anything*, to remain consistent. I mean, why does life always have to be a struggle?
Why can't I just fall into happiness as easily as I fall into her eyes? Why can't *we* fall into happiness? Why should the past come in like the tide and wash away the present, reminding us of all the pain we have experienced and empowering logic to sabotage the opportunity to create something new; something beautiful?

You can help someone over a hurdle in their life, but if they don't learn to jump, you leave them worse off then before; with a new hurdle in front *and* one behind them.
All we can hope to do for others is to empower them because eventually—if they don't discover that all the power comes from within them, they will hold you responsible for how they feel and you will resent yourself.

Most people feel powerless when they discover it takes effort to change; it takes letting go. Letting go—even of the things that no longer serve us, makes us feel unstable.
We tend to blame others for making us feel powerless, hoping to deflect our own sense of responsibility for choices we have made and choices we must make but have prolonged.
Don't look in a mirror if you are not prepared to see your own reflection. Don't smash the mirror for showing you the truth.

One of my biggest challenges has been learning to set boundaries. I invest a lot of myself in the people who are significant to me and inevitably, attach myself to them and the outcomes I set.
We always have expectations. There is no point denying that, just acknowledge those expectations for being what they are and don't allow them to become your truth. How will you recognize your outcomes if you can't admit you set them?
Don't tell stories that support expectations you have developed from past experience.

Every action has a reaction. When others feel that expectations have been placed upon them, they withdraw. When others withdraw, it feels like rejection. The reaction to that is never good.

I have been learning not to give my power away. I am learning that investing in people means being there when it counts, not building an identity around them. Identity, like identification—the ID, comes from within. As soon as you start outsourcing how you see yourself to others, you give all your power away. You become a victim of the story you tell yourself about how others see you because they are not treating you the way you would—the way you think they should, and your mood becomes like polished lava rocks washed in and out with the force of tides you have no control over.

I have this tendency to try and express consciously what I am experiencing subconsciously. This makes me seem self absorbed, which is ironic because I always saw my father as being selfish, and I hated him for that.

THE ISLAND

Ambitious Were The Plans We Laid

As the sun begins to rise, we are crossing the field between the village of houses without roofs and a hill which rises gracefully in front of us. This is a side of the island I have never been, yet it feels familiar and I get a sense of what comes next.

At times the child's hand is in mine. At others, mine in theirs. We are staggered—they are in front, I am wandering behind. Then it's the other way.
I am not sure if what is happening is a dream or a memory; in the past, present or future. Time has lost all relevance to me. We may have been walking for days or hours. It makes little difference.
We arrive at the hill and as I begin to climb I notice my clothes are transforming. I never actually noticed what I was wearing before this, or I don't remember.
I am now dressed in what looks like scales of white leather and iron.

There are three large stones at the top of the hill. Two are standing; the third lies across the top, forming a kind of doorway.
I am standing between the stones looking out over the ocean. The child is no longer with me; I don't know when they left. *My bothers* is circling above me; wings shimmering in the afternoon sun.
The sun becomes the moons and the moons become the sun and the sun becomes the moons. They reflect off the crystal blue water revealing a pyramid with strange symbols just below the surface. *Symbols we were looking for. Symbols on the houses without roofs. Symbols from the fields of sand and land of no water.*

The moons become the sun and the sun becomes the moons and the moons become the sun.

I am walking down the hill towards the crystal blue water and the sun becomes the moons.
The ocean has inhaled and I step onto exposed ocean floor that slopes down sharply. I make my way to an opening at the bottom of the pyramid, and crawl inside.
A great chamber is illuminated by the moonlight. The pyramid appears to be hollow; its walls rising up to a point.
There is a platform in the middle of the room with something on it. I walk forwards and step onto it. There is a device. A kind of navigational instrument. When I place my hand on it, the walls of the pyramid light up with stars and planets and moons and swirling colors.
Many universes surround me. I can see into them all. There are no dimensional barriers.

You open your eyes. You are lying in the sand. In that special place that is always wet, where the ocean exhales.
To your right is the ocean, to my left—the jungle.

I've Come To Resemble My Own Shadow

I am sitting at a kitchen table. The room is full of people talking amongst themselves.
I hear music from the garage. The door is open and sounds pours in.

We live our lives like they are a film or a novel. The people I meet are like characters in my story and I am a character in theirs. It's our mutual agreement. I will never really know them and they will never really know me. We'll only ever know the story we tell ourselves.
I get up from the table and wander through the house. I am looking for someone.
How did I get here? Who did I come with? How long have I been here?

When I open my eyes I am naked in a bathtub. Covered in ice cubes.
I lift myself out and walk downstairs. Sun shines through the window and makes the place look different. In the front room someone is playing guitar. I sit down on the floor, light a cigarette and listen to him sing. My eyes are heavy and I allow them to close.
I become aware of myself floating through space. It is so peaceful and I am so calm. Stretched out before me are the lines of a grid. I am hovering above a kind of intersection where the lines extend into space in all directions. A voice speaks, permitting me to ask any question I like. When I do, a point of light moves along the grid—vertically and horizontally. I follow, suspended in space above it.
The point of light rests at a junction in the grid and instantly I have the answer to my question.
"Ask another, if you like," the voice says, and I do.

Time becomes irrelevant. Someone from the physical world is trying to remove a glass from my hand. I can feel it happening but am still in space. I am still hovering above the grid. My fingers are frozen around the glass. I am afraid that the slightest sensation of awareness within my physical body will jeopardize what is happening.

All around you are people caught up in jobs and control dramas and relationships that are slowly eating away at them. They act powerless to change any of it but the truth is they are too afraid. They are scared of losing what they already have for the uncertainty of gain.
No one was born powerless, we make ourselves that way.

Finally someone rouses me from my vision. I am surprised to learn that I have been sitting this way for hours.

WARRIOR

Only When You're Gone

She is a daughter of Roslyn.
I thought I came to build a chapel. To leave my father and my complacent mother and slowly going mad sister and the memory of my brother far behind me, but *this* is why I have come. *She* was my purpose for leaving.
We fall into one another's eyes.

She leads me through the Glenn and into the faerie forest. We sit for hours without speaking, in the clearing between the doorway trees. I walk to the stream that passes alongside the trees. *My love* walks up behind me. I reach down and pick up a stone. It splits in two in my hand. Right down the center.
We each take half.

I don't know how much time passes. Time has accelerated. Her father wants her to get married. Their families have known each other and it has always been assumed this union would happen. She tells me one day in the faerie forest.
"I don't know that I have any answers for you. If I did, I hope I would keep them to myself. You know how I feel. If you don't, than nothing I can say is going to make it any clearer."
"I know how you feel," she responds. "Sorry if I said too much."
"Honesty is never too much. The moment you keep the truth hidden from me is the moment we lose whatever connection we have."
"I don't want to lose it. I love you. I don't want to be without you, not even for a moment."

NAVIGATOR

Some Bitter Awakening This Has Been

I step outside the door and begin walking. It has been raining all morning and smells of rebirth. *I have never thought of that before, what rain smells like.*
I start down the sidewalk, stepping through puddles as if crossing the Red Sea.

I am nearly struck by a car as I make my way across the street. The driver isn't even looking.
My steel toed boots easily dent the front of his car as I unleash a flurry of misdirected anger.

I am a wreck. I am on the verge if losing it. What am I supposed to do with these memories? All I want is some consistency in my life. Everyone expects it from me but doesn't seem to notice that I may need the same thing. They're not listening back.
Every day I wake up unsure if this is the reality I want to live in, or am intended to. I feel like a displaced traveler trying to find his way back home.

My life is like a starry sky without constellations. If I knew how to string them together then everything would make sense but all I've got is a lot of bright moments that don't seem to weave together.
I've got a simple need that no one seems to understand. It's very hard to get around.

It's raining hard and no one will leave their vehicle. They stare blankly in the rain like wet soppy mops, afraid to intervene because I am taking out my anger passionately, and a thing like passion can't be stopped. It's like the force of entanglement. The other member of the entangled pair will always have a correlated reaction.

The front of his car is good and smoked. I walk up the length of the hood and rip off the drivers side mirror. As I am about to toss it through his window, the driver decides it is a good time to accelerate. Guess he's had enough.

SINISTER

You Came From Somewhere Special

I step into a round room. I think its an astronomy dome. It must be because all around me are stars and planets and swirling colors. The walls are glass and I realize that what I am seeing is outside. Perhaps I am in a lighthouse. I don't know.

I am wearing tall leather boots and the kind of pants an officer would wear. At my waist, beneath my coat, I can feel two revolvers.

A table runs the length of the dome. On it are navigational charts. There is a kind of giant telescope mounted in the glass. I walk over to it. I look around the dome to try and get a better understanding of where I am. *If I am supposed to be here.*
There is a picture frame on the desk. I walk over to it. *My Love.*
I recognize her immediately. She always looks the same to me.

THE ISLAND

When The Claws Come Out

I am ankle deep in the water. I can see the raft. I take a few more steps and dive into the crystal blue water. I swim out to the raft and lift myself onto it.
I open the box. Inside are all my fears. I lift them out and they float into the air with all the emotions attached to those fears and all the memories I associate with them.
Nostalgia won't work against me. I refuse to hang on to these things which no longer serve me. These things are not my identity. If I believe they are, it makes being objective a struggle. Maybe even impossible.
If my identity is tangled in things outside of myself, I will never want to let go. *Release. Let Go. Reborn.*

Sometimes I get tangled in other people; in the ideas of how they will change my life. I set outcomes and become disappointed when my future is not the story I tell myself it should be. This is when the claws come out.

I close my eyes and when I open them again I am sitting about fifty feet below the summit of the volcano, facing east. I look out at the ocean, stretching as far as the horizon.
Around me is a small garden. Time accelerates.
I stand up and begin walking to the summit. There is a stone staircase and I climb it. There are only eight steps and when I reach the last one I notice a pool of water. I walk over and dip my toes inside. The water is as cold as ice. I lower my entire body into it. I even allow my head to sink.
I resurface in the ocean. I am swimming towards the raft with the box on it. I notice someone already on the raft. *My love.*

I climb onto the raft and open the box. I place inside all the things that are weighing me down. All the things that could prevent me from enjoying these moments we are about to share.
Our bodies shoot into the air like missiles. We fly to a rocky bluff, separated from the island when the tide comes in. It looks like a giant came along and removed a slice of rock, creating this separation.
Burrowed into the sides of the bluff are many caves. We walk along the bluff, fifty feet above the crystal blue water. At the far end, a door hangs suspended in the air. An old creaky wooden door. I hover off the ground and pass through the door. I don't open the door, I pass *through* it.
I am a little surprised that I didn't end up somewhere else. Then I turn around.

I see a lot of boats in the water. People are traveling between a chain of smaller islands that now surround the island. In the sky are flying machines unlike any I have seen before.
I travel higher into the air, with *my love.*

I open my eyes. I am on the raft. It is night. I am alone and floating far from the island. The moons are full and their light is the only reason I can see the island at all.
I wonder what happened to *my love.*

Where has she gone? Why can't I find her?
Because you are not looking.
Of course I am looking.
You are not looking in the right place or in the right way.
What does that even mean?
You are neglecting yourself. Start taking care of yourself and she will find you. Don't imagine that anything you do strategically will influence what I bring into your life. Do you trust me?
Of course I trust you.
Do you believe I bring things into your life?
Or course I do.

If you believe I bring things into your life, you must also trust the shape they come. You can't decide when to trust and when not to. The moment you try and control what I have brought into your life is the moment you risk losing it.

SERGEANT

We Both Go Down Together

One of my favourite childhood books was called The Pets Revolt.
It was about all the pets and all the mice in the walls of an apartment building who devise a plan to escape. They collect toilet and paper towel rolls and paper clips and string and build a tunnel through the walls so they can escape, and they do.
I always thought it ended a little prematurely. I wanted to know how they did after they escaped. If they found what they were looking for or discovered something worse, and wished they could return.

ASCENSION

"They say you die twice. Once when you stop breathing and a second time, a bit later on, when somebody says your name for the last time."

Bansky

CONQUERER

Put Your Armour On, Again

I never considered leaving the black rock castle or that *my love* may have a desire for anything but me and this kind of paradise we have created.
Often I watch her—standing on the rocks with the wind blowing through her maze of tangled hair, gazing across Oceans Gate.
She has no memory of the life she lived before this; of the hill across the water where we lost our daughter and she breathed her last. Perhaps if she remembered, she would not secretly desire to leave this place, but I don't tell her anything. I can't. I wouldn't want to introduce that kind of sadness.
Fate has spared her a greater mourning and there is a kind of grace in forgetting. Unless you are the one being forgotten.
I join *my love* on the rocks. She falls into my eyes and takes all her pent up longing and desire out on my body.

She will not remain content on this prison forever. I can't allow my logic to determine what is best for her. It must be the heart that navigates. Her heart as well as mine.

Some things are inevitable, I suppose. Eventually fate will force our hand despite my resolve. I don't know if this is the case or simply my self-loathing, having caught up to me.
We lay on the rocks under the blanket sky, stars too numerous to count. *My love* lies on my body; her head on my chest.

"Have you a desire to leave this place?" I offer. She lifts her head with expressions of surprise and delight.

"I have watched you gazing across Oceans Gate. There is a look of yearning in your eyes as though you wonder if there is something out there for you and you wish to explore it."
"What is it like?" she asks.
"It is a violent world. A cruel place that will eat you alive if given the chance."
She looks into my eyes sadly.
"It is also delightful—filled with many wonders, pleasures and the treasures of experience."
"Do you think it's possible to leave?" she asks.

I don't want to. I think it is a mistake and the very thought of it is like ripping away the last of my armour and sending me out to war, but I don't say this and secretly I wonder if I am sabotaging myself, exhausted from the inner turmoil. At times like this, self preservation works against us.

"I think if we don't try, I may lose you. I am not entirely certain you would not find a way to leave me."
She does not respond—just allows it hang there, but we are thinking the same thing. If I try and keep her here, she will only resent me. I will have become her captor and that would be a worse fate than losing what we have.

NOGWAL

I Will Fall Like A Star

I am surrounded by the swirling colors that identify this place. I open my eyes as planets and stars take shape around me.
I await visions that accompany my presence here; glimpses into lives past and ones to come.

I am sitting on a throne. We are in Egypt. *My love* is standing to one side. Koal around her eyes, desire on her breath. On my other side, the wolf.
In front of me is some kind of navigational instrument. I place my hand on it and instantly we find ourselves projected through the psychedelic tunnel. It smells of rain. The smell of rebirth.

I emerge before a cluster of trees. It is night and from within the trees many pairs of eyes watch me. Either they are glowing or they reflect my light.
I don't know who they are or what this means and am a little terrified.
My body shoots into the air.

We Will Know What Was Right To Do

There is a thought that terrifies me. It keeps me awake at night when I should be dreaming. It eats away at hope and makes my insides churn. This is what fear does. It grabs hold of us and pulls apart what has been woven together. Given the chance, our fears will destroy us mercilessly.

On this journey I have had to confront the lengths at which I will go. Am I willing to learn? At all costs? What am I willing to give up?
The willingness to accept change is a great challenge. Am I willing to change the way I think? What I do? How I act?
Would I let go of how I imagine the outcome to be and embrace the uncertainty of gain?

If I want things in my life to change, I must change things in my life.
The thought terrifies me as much as it does you. I don't know the outcome. Admitting this is the first step. What I know is right now. The objective is in front of me.
This is the only way to proceed. The only way to get things done.

THE ISLAND

Archetype

Where do you see yourself?
My eyes take a moment to adjust. My vision is blurry and I become aware that I am standing in the fog at the top of a volcano. The crater stretches out in front of me, fog descends into its depths. You are cold and my naked body is covered only by a blanket of fur.
Amidst the sharp stones at my feet, a single flower has grown.
I want a better view. I want to see where I am in all its breathtaking entirety.
Instantly you shoot into the air. I pick a direction and travel through the pink clouds.
Now I see the volcano. You see the white sandy beach and the blue crystal water. I can see the bluff that separates from the island when the tide comes in, and the hill with the great stones on top.

I am back on the volcano, breathing in the cool morning air. I walk towards the crater and follow a path that leads into it. I disappear into the fog.
How long I walk, I do not know. I become aware that the ground beneath my feet is changing. I am walking through grass now. It tickles my ankles.
Either the fog is rising or I am going beneath it. I am surrounded by trees, following a path through the forest. It winds deeper and deeper into the volcano.
I hear the sound of running water. I smell smoke and hear the crackling of wood. Ahead of me is a fire.

There is no one waiting for me when I reach it. I sit down on a log and remove the fur that I am wearing. The heat feels good on my skin.

I look through the fire—into the forest, and see her. She is hovering just above the ground. She is wearing a white veil over her face and a shimmering translucent garment.
As she moves out of the trees, I become aware of a cord stretching out from the center of my chest. It passes through the fire and is attached to her throat.

On the ground beside you is a pouch. Inside I will find a tool.
I reach my hand inside. *A measuring stick? How is this going to help me?*
I examine the notches along its edge.
I become aware of many voices crying out from within her. I can see them trying to dig their way out of her stomach.

I look into her veiled face. With the measuring stick in my hand, I gently tap the cord attached to my chest. The cord stiffens and begins to change color—a color that mimics the measuring stick. This transformation moves along the cord to her throat.
A cloud of smoke is released from her mouth. The transformation continues throughout her body. The notches from the measuring stick form geometric shapes on her skin.
Suddenly I lift off the ground as the cord pulls us together. Our bodies meet in the center of the fire but the flames do not burn me. We pass through one another and—as if we are one body, shoot hundreds of feet into the air and begin to circle the island.

We are standing side by side on the white sandy beach with the washed up lava rocks and the crystal blue water. I am standing with *my love.* Above us, the dragonflies circle, humming. *Our bothers.*
We enter the water and swim towards the raft. Our bodies pass through one another with ease. *This is who we are. This is what we were made for.*

I don't know if *my love* was the one I encountered in the volcano; the one wearing the veil. Whatever happened in there was meant to teach me something. I suppose I will figure it out when I wake up.

WARRIOR

LEAVE US ONLY WITH A SONG

We have smeared our faces in mud and the blood of our enemies.
The sun is not yet risen and we stand together on the battlefield. My brother and best friend, at my side.
All the rage and anger and destruction inside me is about to explode.
And then it begins. We are running towards the enemy. Weapons in our hands.
I run with tears in my eyes. I run for all the pain I must endure. I run recklessly and with abandon, knowing some things are inevitable. No amount of mourning and empathy can fix this useless helpless feeling.
My sword falls down hard on his head.
In every direction floods a symphony of blood and organs. We tear living bodies open and ravage the dead.

Time accelerates. I wait for her in the clearing between the doorway trees.
How long I am waiting, I can't say. It begins to snow. I lay down.
I close my eyes and find I am nearly weightless. I am not in my body.
I am ascending through the trees, flying above the fields towards the coast. Past the hill where *my love* breathed her last; across the violent waters of Oceans Gate and the black rock castle—spit out of the sea in rebellion. Beyond the borders of this land and into another.

I open my eyes to the sound of wedding bells ringing across the Glenn; from the chapel I came here to build.
My love is here. She lies on top of me and lays her head on my chest. Our roots relax. We are tangled.

Inside my boot is a dagger. She reaches for it with my logical arm. She is singing a charming kind of lullaby; a sacrifice offered up for what she is about to do. Her voice haunts me already.
She kisses me softly and—with a final gesture of resignation, allows her fingers to brush across my cheek, tracing the lines and feeling my warmth a final time.

NAVIGATOR

The Universe Will No Longer Support Us In Being Small

You recognize the cluster of trees in front of me. *I have been here before.*
There were people hiding in the trees. Their eyes glowed. They were terrified. *I was terrified.* The fear caused me to run away. I won't do that again. There is something that needs to be done.

GOEL is with me. As we circle the trees, I look into the midst of them—not with my physical eyes, but my other eyes.
They are still here. They are still terrified. *They have been waiting here so long.*
"You don't need to remain in this prison of your own making. You can leave here. You can leave now. You only need to let go of what you are holding onto—the memories haunt you like ghosts."

I have been thinking about patterns in my life. It's pretty hard to avoid this when I see them every time I close my eyes.
History teaches us that man learns absolutely nothing from history. Many have died waiting for a glitch is this pattern.
History doesn't change itself. We change history. To do this, we must become aware of the patterns.

Self awareness shines a light on how the events of our experience become the identity patterns that shape the story of ourselves we believe. This is the source point that must be adjusted if we want to change things.

Muscles are points of decision making that tell us if we are storing tension. Tension will compress the energy that allows body systems to function. If the systems are working in harmony, your emotions will stabilize.
The body is a laboratory; a kind of universe of its own. 100,000 chemical reactions are taking place in every cell every second. Emotions are chemicals put into motion by our choice to react or respond.
Communication between cells happens faster than the speed of light. 10 million cells die per second and are instantly replaced.
Establishing new patterns can happen as effortlessly as this. Once you realize that we are constantly in a state of reinvention, the idea of being bound to patterns and belief systems, dissolves.

We filter the actions of others through our own perspective. No matter how much you do to empathize with people, you won't succeed by talking at them or trying to convince them you have their answers. They must come to realize the answers are within them.
Listen and respond and if absolutely necessary, use words. The impulse to speak reflects your desire to make everything about you. I do this because I seek approval.

To reach the peak of confidence, one must first climb a mountain of insecurity.
Stand in your truth. The confidence in you will assure others of your authenticity. Don't assume you know others better than they know themselves. They will resent you and build walls of protection around themselves; great chasms for which no bridge exists to take you to the other side.
Admit the things that make you happy. Admit you don't have all the answers and give others the credit for discovering their own.

The beauty of this adventure we call life is relationships; the co-creation of learning. Embrace the people in your life and love without conditions.
The most amazing things come to us without our interference. We aren't required to fight for the things we desire most, only be willing to not have them. I must be willing not to have her; not to have her in the way I want.

It often takes being on the brink of total annihilation to realize the value of what we comfortably neglect.
There is a difference between casting blame and taking responsibility.
There is a difference between influence and control.
Be honest with yourself and give your intention to love, and all will go well for you.

THE ISLAND

Did I Talk In My Sleep

I am standing on a rock shelf next to a waterfall. Towering above me is the volcano. I listen to the sounds from the jungle. I turn and look below me, towards the white sandy beach with the washed up lava rocks.
At some point I move towards the waterfall. I begin climbing the rocks behind the water.
I lift myself onto a plateau. The water flows calmly here, before gravity takes over.
I walk along the stream, stopping at intervals to soak in the beauty of this place. I am full of gratitude.

There is a wall of trees about thirty feet away. Thick like hedges. The stream flows from within their roots. I run my hand along their intricately woven life and suddenly I feel a door. A door within the trees. It opens easily and I walk through.

It is night and I am leaning against a tree. In front of me a fire rages. The tree has grown in the middle of the stream, meters away from where gravity takes over.
The moons are full. Their light illuminates the sky and ocean. The jungle remains dark, though its canopy is bathed in a soft glow.
How long I sit here, I can't say. I stare into the flames and feel light-headed. I feel exhausted. My body is sweating and I feel disoriented. I am dizzy because my spirit hasn't fully connected with my body. It is with *my love.*

I hear a humming above me. *My bothers.*

I stand and walk past the fire. I step towards where the water falls down. Below me is a valley. I never noticed this before. The valley leads to the bluff that is separated from the island when the tide comes in.
Is this where I am intended to go?
I step off the ledge.
Instead of falling hundreds of feet, my body moves through the sky—towards the moons.

The closer I get to the twin moons, the more they draw together. Their edges seem to sink into the surface of one another. *Cosmic entanglement.*
There is a kind of inverted eye shaped doorway where the moons have joined. I am moving towards this.

I stand inside the doorway and my eyes become very heavy. I close them and when I open them I am lying on the purple bed, on the white sandy beach.
The sun is out but the moons are still visible.

I love seeing the moons in daytime. They remind me how big the universe is, and how small the issues I make big, really are.
Where is *my love*? I tilt my head and see her lying on the purple bed, but in another place. Another sequence of time. She is in the city of stone and health and separation.
I am transported there. She slips her hand inside my hand and we are instantly back on the island, next to one another on the purple bed.
I sit up and hold my hands over her mostly sleepy body. I can feel the energy from my palms escape into her and am consumed with visions from other times; times that are happening at this very moment. I am visiting the memories you have stored in your tissue. I see it all. I see all the pain and pleasure and the reason you are sick. I try to pull it out like a string but I can't. I can't do anything for you but let go.
You say something, then, in your sleep. I am startled because I don't expect it.

SATORI

The People You Wish To Remove Yourself From

I open my eyes in a sea of pink clouds. I am moving or being moved along very quickly. At times the clouds are thin enough that I can make out blue sky and infinite number of strings that seem to hold reality together.

I feel an overwhelming sensation I cannot explain. I am both warm and cold, shivering and peaceful—all at the same time.

I look above me and see *my bothers.* Suddenly I become aware that we are traveling to the center.

"I don't understand," I speak aloud as if I need to use words.

"This is her body."

I look through the clouds again and below me is a field. A field I have been to before. *I have been here many times. In many forms.*

I tilt my head a little and the field becomes flesh. *My love.*

Suddenly the overwhelming sensation—the hot and cold, the shivering and peaceful, make sense to me; like my entire being is one the verge of some great orgasm and it makes me dizzy as we travel through the clouds and along your skin.

I am consumed with questions I don't understand how to ask.

As if responding to these thoughts, the voice speaks again.

"When you try to understand, you make this about you, and this is not about you."

My vision begins to blur and I am transported somewhere else. The voice continues to speak.

"This is Satori."

I am standing on the ledge of a building so tall I cannot see the ground. All I see are more pink clouds many floors below me.
"Release and let go. You will be reborn. Fall into this."
I jump off the ledge and begin falling. I am falling faster than my body—like the sensation of the higher self departing. I open my arms wide as I descend towards the pink clouds. I hear *my love* speak to me from somewhere. I don't know where.
"Most of all I need you."

I am standing on a rolling staircase leading into an aircraft. As I pass through the door I notice *my love*, steps ahead of me. She turns around and we embrace, excited with our growing success. *We are becoming proficient at this.*
It is a small aircraft. A private jet. We recognize the other people. They travel with us. *They travel with us.*
We take our seats. The jet takes off and we are flying through pink clouds.
I get up and move to the back of the jet; into the restroom. A moment later, *my love* follows me.

I leave the bathroom first. We are on a different jet. It is a huge airliner. The ones with a six person isle sandwiched between smaller isles on the side.
The jet is full of people we know, like the seating arrangement at a wedding; yours to the right, mine to the left. I walk back to my seat staring at all these faces, trying to anticipate the reason things have changed.

Within moments of sitting down, the bathroom door opens and you step out. Suddenly the plane shakes in the air.
The oxygen masks drop down. I rise to my feet, instinctively, and see you clutching the top of a chair. I grab my mask and put it on—the cool oxygen flowing deep into my cylinder.

As the turbulence continues, I begin to notice the reactions of people. Some are in a complete panic. Others seem indifferent.

I am calling you with my eyes. You are struggling your way down the isle when someone calls your name. They ask you to help them put their mask on.
There is no reason they can't do it themselves and I am a little frustrated when you stop and help them. . . . *place your own mask on before you assist others.*
I am calling you with my eyes and *our bothers* are humming loudly in response.
Another person calls for you to help them. I can't understand your hesitation.
You look at me pleadingly, and now more people—seeing your willingness to do for others what they can do for themselves, begin calling out, wailing for you to help them.
I can see the conflict on your face. I realize that you have forgotten we are dreaming. You have been pulled in. I take off my oxygen mask and begin running up the isle towards you. I know that when I touch you, you will remember again and we can make this dream end. I think we have learned the intended lesson of this adventure.
As I am running, I trip on something and—hitting the ground, my vision goes hazy.

A YOUNG PRINCE IN DISQUISE

I'll Be Joining With Them Soon

We are nearly finished our journey, and rest in a mostly dried up river bed. My horse is drinking from a stream. GOEL wanders nearby. We have reached our destination.
In front of me—on a hill, stand the remains of a great stone structure. The only part of it left intact is a tower, beaten and worn by the wind and rain and time.
Inside is *my love.*
This is why we have come. My purpose is nearly complete. I have come to free her from this place.

I leave my body and rise into the sky. Below me I can see my human suit and my horse drinking and GOEL running. I float towards the tower; towards the solitary window. As I approach, I see *my love* inside. She cannot see me.
I pass through the window and come to rest on the floor behind her.
She is sitting on a chair, in front of a mirror. She is holding a brush and runs it through her long maze of hair.
I stare into the mirror and see tears on her saddened face. I listen to her thoughts and embody her pain. This is why I have come.

Outside the physical body, I can hear her emotions speak. She feels abandoned by everyone, alone in this tower. Waiting for something to happen that will change her life. Waiting for *someone to happen* that will change her life. Waiting and feeling abandoned. Waiting to be married.
I want to tell her that all of the strength she needs is inside her. And if she could realize the power contained within her, that she could be free from this place and the sickness that has become her prison. This

physical tower is simply a metaphor. Nothing is keeping her here. All she has to do is leave.
But words aren't the answer. They won't remedy the situation.
This is the only way to love her.

Beneath her skin—just below the shoulders, wrapped around her bones like bracelets, are the black marks of her disease; a disease that will spread through her body and eat her alive from the inside if she does not leave this tower and the ghosts that haunt her.
I step in close. I place my hands over the bracelets of disease. I feel the energy transfer from my palms into her. I feel the disease unwrap from her bones and move into my palms like liquid. It moves into my hands and begins traveling up my arms.
My body grows weaker and I am dizzy. The disease wraps itself around my bones, like bracelets.

I am staring into the mirror. Her eyes are closed and the muscles in her face begin to relax.
Suddenly she is staring at me. *She can see me. She can see what I am doing.* For a moment, time becomes irrelevant and we are lost in one another's eyes. Every memory we have ever shared is relived. We can see it all and we experience it all. *I have spent my life preparing for this moment. She is watching for my peace. She must see the ease in me.*
When the moment is over, I am gone. I am gone with all the ghosts that haunt her and move through her like the tide, depositing the past like washed up lava rocks into the present; devouring hope of escape.
It won't take her long to forget what was done here today; to forget me. She will leave this prison with the taste of freedom on her lips, not the taste of me. She will begin to lose all of the memories we created; the moments we shared while we journeyed through the timestreams.
Her life will continue as if I never existed at all.

As my body ascends toward the Nogwal, I am graced with a kind of mourning. I am sad, but this is not a terrible kind of mourning. I mourn because I am not with her; that we couldn't share this life together, yet a strong love and strange peace overwhelm me. I refused to be her captor inside a prison of my expectations and outcomes. I succeeded where I have failed before. I changed history. I am integrating the lessons. I am learning. This was the only way she could be free, and I am going to a place where I can watch her until we are reunited once again.

I will imagine you are here with me, entangled in consciousness. Surrounded by planets and stars and swirling colors, I will express gratitude for the reserve of calm that graced me enough to give you back your truth and transition in peace.

NAVIGATOR

Does It Make Sense In Your Eyes?

She stands in front of the fountain, facing me.
None of the hesitation that exists in the world of stone and health and separation, exists here. We have no inhibitions. We just live.
There is no need to rationalize or justify any other impulse than what is the most authentic expression for how we are feeling.
We are completely void of judgement. That comes later, after we wake up.

It's a terrible thing to go through life judging ourselves, by the way we assume others see us, and the way we see ourselves.
I don't want to live that way. I can't. Not anymore.

I am lying in bed. On the loft under the twin moons. I am not fully back, lingering between worlds. I am dizzy because my spirit hasn't fully connected with my body because it is with *my love.*
I am surrounded by light beings. Without speaking, they tell me they are here to help me remember; to quicken the process because we are running out of time.
One of them touches my communication toe. They tell me this will help me speak my truth.
My vision begins to blur and when I refocus my eyes, I am at a kitchen table.
Sitting across from me is *my love.* I don't recognize this place, yet it feels familiar. It feels like the most important thing I can do is remember this. Like maybe all the answers I am seeking originate from here.

There has got to be a point of original creation for which all other realities mimic. And the choices made in *that* reality, must affect them all.
I am witnessing the source point. This is original creation. But where is here and how do I return to it?

Someone speaks. I turn my head. Our daughter. *Our daughter—God of the New World.*
""What the hell is going on, mom?!"

When I open my eyes, the light beings are gone. It is early in the morning. My eyes are heavy and I don't want to get up. I don't want to leave. *My love* is still here. I am dizzy because my spirit hasn't fully connected with my body.
This happens. This is what we do.

THE DESERT

Will You Come See Me In The Morning

In the desert the sun feels closer to the earth. The heat feels like flames of fire that dance within reach of your skin. Heat that makes your head swim. The kind of disoriented feeling that pain leaves you with. The kind of pain you need because it points things out, but the kind of pain that can't be trusted because sometimes pain lies.

I have been here before, with *my love*. We search the desert for ancient symbols. She wears koal around her eyes and her hair is painted black. We have come here in other times as well. We know this. We travel together. We move through the timestreams, acting out different roles. Always searching for one another. Searching even if we don't know we are searching. And when we find each other, we begin remembering. We remember what we already know. All the memories we have collected together. All the pain and sorrows and happiness and ecstasy.
There is always a challenge. Some new thing we must learn. The role we play reveals the challenge and what we do once we have identified the challenge is how we integrate the lesson.

We are traveling with a caravan. Looking for symbols. Always looking for symbols. And we always sleep in a tent with many purple pillows.
I feel light headed and disoriented.

Lately I have been coming to the desert alone. The desert is the kind of place that makes you feel pain in extreme ways.

We tell ourselves a story that pain is something that can be trusted; an impartial teacher. But sometimes we manifest our own pain. This is when it can't be trusted.

I am not walking. I am inside an orb, floating through the desert. I didn't mention that? Sorry, I should have mentioned that first.

Through the residue of heat that hangs like fog, I see a bridge ahead. Why there is a bridge in the desert I don't know, but there it is. I question if this is simply a mirage. I consider walking onto it and falling because it doesn't really exist, but sometimes everything is exactly what it seems. Sometimes a mirage is like a story I tell myself that isn't real.

The bridge is an enormous structure or maybe it just seems this way because it is in the desert and nature does not outweigh its grandness. Not that the desert isn't grand, but it's a lot of the same. Fields of sand without distractions, so when you see something like a bridge, it seems bigger than it would somewhere else.

The bridge is constructed of great wooden beams, with jade inlaid trim. It is a walking bridge—the width of three men, with railings on the side just above waist height.
I can't even see the length of it, or maybe my eyes haven't adjusted yet.

Now I see. I still have a ways to travel on this bridge, but there are large doors at the end. This heightens my expectation. I don't really know what to expect, and I try to avoid imagining what I will find on the other side of the doors. That only leads to disappointment. I know that every step is a step towards home.

When I reach the far end, I find myself in front of large wooden doors. They are also inlaid with jade. They have got to be thirty feet high. There is nothing beyond these doors that I can see, just more fields of sand, but I have come to realize that there doesn't need to be.
I reach my hand out and touch the door. I step outside the orb, knowing it has brought me here; where I need to be. *My bothers* circles above. I can tell by the pitch of his hum that this is the right direction. *My love.*

I would be lying if I said I don't have regrets, but regrets don't have to be a bad thing. Regrets teach us how to make better decisions. They remind us that we are responsible for what we do; that every choice counts.
Things in life can get lost without the certainty of finding them again. In order to live, you must cease the struggle to live. Love is not always about letting go, it's about being willing to.
When you hold your breath, time stands still and you become one with yourself and the Divine. Listen to the silence within your own body. And then exhale.

CONQUERER

Our Time Won't Live That Long

I suppose I knew this day would come and it's why I stowed the boat. That was before *my love* arrived on the black rock castle, and since then I neglected the memory.
To be honest, I am pretty content stranded here. The elements can be harsh and we forge our survival by eating fish, fowl, and whatever the tide brings us, but we are happy. We survive. We spend our days swimming and talking and laughing and making love on the rocks. Our nights are spent the same.
Our bothers offer us gracious amusement. We watch them in the sky above. They are content having been reunited. *Why isn't she?*

My biggest concern is the boats that seem to patrol Oceans Gate. There are fishing vessels and there are the ones that make war. Between these and the flying ships, we are not going to get far if they try and stop us. If they don't—and we make it to Sinister, how do we even begin to explain who we are and where we are from?
My memories now begin at the hill across Oceans Gate; the hill where my love breathed her last. I can't even remember my name. I don't know where I came from.

I have considered the possibility that we are not visible to others. After all, we *are* dead. Unless this world we are now a part of is also inhabited by dead people, then they might not be able to see us. Then again, this entire world could be a kind of limbo state; each person assigned to their own prison. And no one escapes without paying the toll.

I am in the cavern, now, staring at the boat, contemplating this decision. If we leave, we will never return. Life will change, and I am not fully convinced I want it to.

NAVIGATOR

I Don't Know How Else To Love You

I spend the whole night jumping in and out of alternates. When I finally make it back to the beach, *my love* is no longer there. The purple bed is in the sand. I climb onto it and close my eyes.

Within a couple hours of waking, I am filled with anxiety. I call them distress calls. I have no idea where they come from—*who they come from*, but it's like being carried by a wave; an extremely fierce wave that eats me alive from the inside.

I am talking to myself. A whole lot of nonsense that won't do me any good.
You know what I'd like? Some consistency. I am supposed to be the strong one—the one that makes everybody feel better, but how do I feel better? Who will be strong for me?
You want to hear about my life? My pain? Of course you don't but let me tell you anyway. Everyone leaves me. They take my strength and suck me dry.
My breath may be shallow but I am still here. I am still alive.

Ok, that's enough. I can't do this to myself. It's time to get back to subjective reality. Pretty soon I will find myself in another place. No need to get fixated on the things I can't change—here in this land of stone and health and separation.
Some things are inevitable, even mandatory self loathing. It reminds us we aren't perfect yet.

Creating scenarios and having imaginary conversations does me no good. It's the power of creation at its most unhealthy and self destructive. I can wind myself up on entirely fabricated stories and have the audacity to act on them. This only succeeds in alienating what I desire most.
I am working towards being whole while feeling like I am missing a limb. It is disorienting, like pain is disorienting.
So what am I supposed to do now? Do you know that my life turned around when I met you? Have I told you that this reality is the one I want to stay in? To be with you and all our collected memories and the new ones we will create?

Today—right now, must become my source point for which all other events mimic. Every choice counts. What I do in this moment determines even what has been done. The power of reinvention is like redeeming layers.

Once it seems like the world is out to get you, it is. Grace seems like judgement because we have done nothing to deserve it and we feel it must cost something. Well, it does cost something. It's not free. There are a lot of conditions. People like to say that grace is free but it's only because they don't have anything intelligent to say, and when people don't know what to say, they settle for a lot of things they don't mean.

Grace allows us to accept circumstance without feeling we need to change it. Authentic love is someone who knows you well enough to tell your story without embellishing it.

"I watched you wake up this morning. I saw you open your eyes."

SINISTER

Burn It To The Ground

I am standing in front of the half moon shaped window, watching *my love*. She looks across the violent waters of Oceans Gate. This memory I hold in my mind, like a photograph. I imagine the wind lightly blowing through her tangled mess of hair. She is beautiful. She has a look on her face. I have seen it before, in this life and many like it. *Why have I been abandoned? Why am I trapped here?*
It occurs to me that these are my own thoughts. These are the stories I tell myself about who I am. Isn't that interesting—we both feel the same way, yet we abandon one another?
I break away from my daydream. I am half dressed and must not waste any more time. I turn around and *my love* is lying on the bed, across the dome shaped room. I grab my shirt off a chair and tuck it into my pants. Then I place two firearms in holsters behind my back.
I walk over to the desk. There is a kind of microscope sitting there and I open a vial and pour some liquid out into a small container. I mix in some powder and let it sit for a few moments. I turn back around and look at *my love*.
What a strange journey this has been. *It always ends this way.*
I lift the small container off the desk. The powder has solidified in the liquid and has formed a wafer. I walk to the purple bed and sit down, placing the wafer on the night stand.

We couldn't afford to create more separation, or make more mistakes. It was becoming harder to find one another. The challenges were proving more difficult to navigate. She was losing her memory. More was required for her to remember; more *is* required. More is required and I don't know what to do.

After I found her, I moved us here—to the black rock castle, spit out of the sea in rebellion. I moved us here to keep her secluded and she feels like a prisoner here.
If she could remember who she was and who she has been, I don't think she would long for escape. I think she would realize this is paradise. *Our opportunity to change things.*
I am not certain how my actions will affect us in the next transition; how they already have. Perhaps I am sabotaging myself, exhausted from the inner turmoil; waking up with these memories, unsure which world I belong, struggling to find answers to questions not yet formed; lessons hidden behind non-adjusted eyes.
At times like this, self preservation works against us.
I reasoned that isolating *my love* was the only way to stimulate her memory. If I lost her, I am not sure we would find one another again and perhaps I would begin losing memories, as well.
There is a kind of grace in forgetting, unless you are the one being forgotten.

There is knock on the door. I take a deep breath. I have known this day would come; have spent my life preparing for this moment; preparing to respond not react. *They will be watching for my peace. They must see the ease in me.* It has taken me a lifetime to arrive at this place.

I am greeted at the door by two officers. They are dressed like me. These are my most trusted aides. I recognize them from collective memories, as if I am already outside the body.
We climb into a kind of hovercraft. Aside from the two pilots, it is just the three of us. The rest of the team is in place on the other side. We are on our way to Sinister to destroy it.
As we depart, I am dizzy. Part of me has stayed behind; with *my love.*

Time accelerates. Explosions are going off and the village is in flames. People are shouting and Sinister is in chaos. I see one of our hovercraft drivers. He is trying to put the flames out with buckets of water. Eventually he gives up. His family is safe. This is the only thing that is important. He realizes this. I see it on his face.

I see my death in a series of hazy lights. I am on a gurney, being pushed through a narrow stone hallway with hanging lights at the top. I am blinking and blinking and suddenly I am out of my body.
I am an observer hovering over Oceans Gate. I witness a bright light shoot into the air. That light is me. *My essence.* The human suit has died, and I race towards the black rock castle. To *my love.*

I stand in the dome shaped room. *My sleeping princess.* She is lying on the purple bed, taking her last breaths. I look at the nightstand. The container is empty. The wafer is gone. She has taken the poison.
Watching her now, there are so many things I wish I would have said. I realize how much I have hurt her in this life. I see what I have done, taking her away from other people, isolating her on the black rock castle. I believed it was the right thing to do, for us. *For me.*
She wasn't well. She was losing her ability to fight. Something had to be done or she would forget completely. *There is a kind of grace in forgetting.*
Everything we have experienced through the timestreams would be lost, and we may never find one another again. I brought her to this prison of my own making and we lived here happily and we lived here miserably—on a moment by moment basis, with moment by moment pain. The kind of pain that eats you alive from the inside. The kind of pain that lies.

I was selfish. If I believe that some force guides me, then I must believe it guides me—it guides *us*, all the time. I can see the pattern, and I am overwhelmed by it. I am always asking so much of her. I treat her like she is the source point for my happiness, and that is unfair.
Something is happening to her mind. She is losing her memory and her will to fight for it. She is tired. She feels lonely; abandoned. How was I unable to see that we feel the same way and that my actions were only reinforcing this belief system within her?
I am consumed by the thought that my actions have made things worse for us; created more separation. I don't know what to do. I don't know what will happen next.
"I don't want you to disappear," I whisper, as tears escape my eyes.
I lie down next to *my love* and cradle her small body in my arms one last time.

I am so lost. I don't know how to love her. *I should have loved you more.*
I fall into all the life and love she has left to offer. I sing a charming kind of lullaby, a sacrifice offered up for what I have already done.
I kiss her softly and with a final gesture of resignation, allow my fingers to brush across her cheek, tracing the lines and feeling her warmth a final time.
Her breath changes.
She inhales deeply. A subtle suggestion that her next one won't be sufficient.
"I am grateful for your every breath. Each one has been a precious gift to me. Now exhale."

NOGWAL

You've Got To Run To The Ones Who Made You

We leave our bodies behind and lift off the bed. We pass through the stone roof and shoot into the air; into the night blanketed with stars too numerous to count.
We become tangled amidst the moonlight.

We are in the Nogwal. The place of rebirth. The comforting womb. The source of all creation. Surrounded by stars and planets and swirling colors, we make love.
Time does not exist in this place, only the reliving of memories, challenges and lessons integrated.
The ultimate act of creation is now alive within her belly.

We are walking on a path through snow capped mountains. *The path that has been laid out for us.*
I feel so much gratitude for this opportunity to be here with *my love.*
How did it begin? The source point of it all?
I cannot recall our life before the timestreams, when we made a mutual agreement to learn together. I don't know why I can't remember this, but there must be a reason. That reason is my hope.
I must find or create hope. What else am I to do? Hope is momentum. Survival depends on it.
I must continue to believe in the love I have experienced. I must continue to believe that it exists, without allowing my past to be the standard for this present reality. History is not bound to repeat itself. I can change things.

This is a time for reflection. Of learning to be silent and appreciate the sympathetic magic that brought me to this place. It brought me here for a reason. I am sure to find this out.
I must keep hope alive, even if hope remains hidden, because the hope of a thing is better than an absolute. Absolutes only satisfy our urge to be in control and only succeed in robbing us of potential.

The path follows precariously along the mountain side. Below us is a valley; a valley I have been to before. *In a different time. In a different place.*
She loses her footing, catching herself on my arm. We share a nervous laugh as the sky grows dark. We continue walking.
I move to stand on the outside. As we exchange places, she slips. This time her fingers cannot grip my sleeve.
I reach out for her.

At times like these, all we can do is hope that self preservation will work for us, not against us. The difference between sympathy and empathy is like the choice to fall into the ravine with her or stay on the path and lower down a rope. The problem is, I'm not sure which is sympathy and which is empathy.

I always considered myself an empath, and I have worn that self imposed title like a badge on my chest. I examine this badge every time I resent myself.
What do I know of empathy? What do I know of another's feelings? All I know are my feelings—how I would feel if it were me in their place, and that is what I project on others. Maybe it's accurate. Maybe it's not.

There comes a point when we realize that the world is different than our own experience; when holding others up to our standards no longer makes sense.
My experience is my own. Perhaps the badge I have been wearing all this time isn't empathy at all, but a badge of mimicry. Mimicking my own feelings. Projecting them on others.
Much less noble. Much less romantic in nature. A lot more masochistic.

But its too late. My love falls over the side, and our daughter—The *God of the New World*, is lost.
Perhaps some things are inevitable.

THE PILOT

How Lucky We Are

Everything will be more than okay, it will be divine. It will be exactly as it is supposed to be, and soon you can write and I'll climb up onto your lap and tell you how lucky we are, and I'll brush the hair out of your face. I'll wipe away the tears, and we will be okay. Everything will be okay Mark William Allard. I am here. I am there and we have been given this gift.

Don't cry! I am not there to wipe away your tears! Hush now, babe, it's all okay. Save it. Write it down and post it above your bed so I am always there and you always know this is my desire—to make everything perfect for you; to nurture you and be your rock. I'm little, physically, but my spirit can wrap itself around you and any burdens you may have. I know it because this is what I do; it's the exact type of thing I do best. I'd be in my little comfy clothes and you will be too. Then I will brew us some tea and we will talk everything out.

CONQEUROR

The Rushing Waves To Bare Our Witness

Ever since I showed *my love* the boat, she has been going down to the cavern. She sits there and looks at it, as if it offers her everything she has ever wanted.
I never thought I could be jealous of an inanimate object.

I would be lying if I said that I have not had a nightmare or two about her leaving without me. I wake up to the high pitched whistle of *my bothers* and find her and the boat, gone. It caused me such a panic that I neglected to show her the boat until only a few days ago.

When there is nothing to do but eat, sleep and make love, you find yourself paying attention to a lot of things you would otherwise take for granted. Things like observing the routines of nature and man.
The fisherman, the war boats, the flying machines—they all operate on a kind of routine that not only makes them predictable, it makes then vulnerable.
Given these observations, I have decided we will leave tomorrow. Perhaps no one will even take notice, but if they are watching us—intent on keeping us prisoners here, then we must leave when they are weakest.

It is still dark when we say our last goodbye to the home we have made—carved into the black rock castle.
We don't have much to bring. Enough food to last us until we can forage for something new. The very thought reminds me how easy we have it here. Plenty of fish and fowl. It will not be as easy on the mainland. There

is bigger game, but more land for them to hide, and others who will be looking for food as well.
I have brought along weapons; the spear I carved out of driftwood that I use to fish, and two revolvers that were in the boat when it drifted in.

Under the cover of darkness we will sail, choosing not to approach Sinister head on, unsure of what we can expect. We will cross to the western bluffs—and from there, circle back to land.
There is a part of me that hopes—even expects, my love to change her mind. Perhaps before we go. Or in route.
Something has to change. I could not live this way, knowing she is not completely satisfied with me; knowing she secretly wishes for an escape. She would always be waiting for it, and I would resent myself for offering a love which is not returned equally.
My loves climbs into the boat, cradling our daughter in her arms. She sits down and I push us off.

We are about a mile from the black rock castle when the attack begins. Boats make towards us from Sinister. Then come the airships.
Very soon we will be surrounded and I don't know what will come next. Will they take us back to the black rock castle or does some greater fate await us? *Separation.*
The air ships begin firing upon us, and now the boats. They mean to destroy us. This is our fate.
If we leave we will never be able to return.

There is no hesitation. I know what I must do. A moment longer could be too late. I am so grateful to have loved her in life and in death, but I will not watch her die again. Not even if I can save myself in the process.
I know that if they kill me first, this opportunity will no longer exist. I don't know how else to love her.
Sometimes self preservation works to destroy us, and it is okay.

As bullets fly through the air around us, I kiss her softly. With a final gesture of resignation, my fingers brush across her cheek, tracing the lines and feeling her warmth a final time.
I throw myself from the boat.

As I sink into the icy waters of Oceans Gate, the last thing I see is my essence—my life force, form a protective orb around *my love* and our daughter, *God Of The New World*. It carries them from the boat, towards the twin moons.
They have become invisible to the boats of Sinister and the war machines that descend from the air.
Circling above the orb that keeps them safe, *our bothers* scream in unison.

As my breath is sustained, rejoice.

NAVIGATOR

BROKEN

"I'm going to try and not sound angry. I am just expressing myself passionately, and a thing like passion can't be stopped."
"It sounds different when you are talking about me. *You* sound different."
"It sounds different because you are giving up. The self awareness you once had is being suffocated by your cowardice."
"When you say things like that, they hurt and I want to shut down."
"You already shut down. Don't put that on me."

"I know my actions are stronger than my words. I am so guilty of that. I never wanted to be another person to cause you pain. We're both trying to have an authentic human experience. No reason to give up. This will make us stronger. We are both sensitive, that's all. We were such in a good place until you let the ghosts back in, and we started to react off one another's reaction. It leaves the situation pretty hopeless. And I feel pretty . . ."
"Powerless?"
"Yea, powerless. Not that I want power, I just want some consistency. I want it to be okay to have hope. I felt the shift—the darkness of where you are going, and it's all panic. You are panicking because you don't feel in control, and I am panicking because I don't feel in control. We have a mess of panic and there is nothing I can do. You are on your own to face the ghosts."
"You felt that?"
"Yea. I get distress calls. Always have. I feel what other people are going through and that is a challenge. And then I beat myself up for doing the wrong thing, because I can't save them. I beat myself up for embodying

their emotion and making it about me. I am learning, though. Learning how to manage it.

It has taken me a lifetime to learn this gift. To learn that it can work for me or against me. To separate dreams and desires and destiny. To silence the chatter of my ego so I can simply *listen.* And set boundaries. I just want to be heard. To have someone listen to me and acknowledge that I have feelings and emotions too. But no one ever does. They just want to be listened to, and right now I am telling myself this is happening again, cause it seems that way. God forbid anyone take a moment to listen to me."

"I never thought it would be horrible to talk to you. That's just a story you tell yourself."

"You're right. I am telling myself a story. But I want more from you than just to talk to me, I want you to listen. I am just so broken."

"Don't ever say that. Don't ever say you are broken."

SATORI

Visions That Plaque Memories

I am in a snow covered field. I feel lonely and then remember GOEL is here with me. Or did he just materialize now?
I wonder why we are back here. *My bothers* is above me. He will show us the way. He always does.
I know that somewhere ahead is the cave. *The cave of my consciousness.*
I don't know if this is where we are headed.
If I knew the future, I would probably try and change it or make it happen right away.
That's a pretty good reason for me not to know the future.

Things are changing. I don't know how, but things are changing. It isn't bad, it just means things are going to be different. Part of me is more at peace. Part of me is in mourning.
I think it's possible to be at peace while mourning. And to be honest, a part of me is even giddy—perhaps because I am sabotaging myself, exhausted from the inner turmoil. At times like this, self preservation can work against me.

Sometimes we need change to happen so desperately, we create it; even if it means making bad decisions. Often when we make decisions to change things, they never look the same, and that's not always bad. The voice of fear is opposite from the voice of inspiration.
Sometimes things get lost, without the certainty of ever finding them again.
Love is not about letting go, it's about being willing to. But sometimes it's about letting go.

We arrive at the entrance to the cave. I am filled with anxiety. I have been feeling this way for a while.
I hesitate at the entrance, knowing GOEL will not follow me in. This is about me. The sky has grown dark and it has begun to snow.
"How else do you expect to understand love?"

I step into the cave.

I am consumed with incredible nausea. I fall to the ground and feel like someone is pouring acid on my back. I start vomiting and my body shakes violently. I can't catch my breath. I feel I am about to die and I don't want to die this way—inside a prison of my own making.
This cave represents more than my consciousness, it represents the story of myself I believe. As long as I believe I am in a prison—as long as I believe that history is doomed to repeat itself, it will.

My head begins to throb. My stomach is eating itself. Memories dig themselves out from my stomach; from the casket shaped reality I have created for them; fingers bleeding and caked with blood and splinters. I can feel my skin burning. I become aware of my third eye; then I pass out.

I am an observer, watching my alternate self experience, but unable to *feel* it; revisiting events as though watching old silent films I have seen before.
Maybe the real learning begins when I stop trying to participate and just let it happen. Just watch and listen.

The answers are in the guidelines. *Guide* lines. Did you get that? The things that guide us. We will know what we should do if we are paying attention to how we are being guided. If we act independently of that, we have only ourselves to blame, because things will never go as we plan unless we are doing what we are intended to.
We must be willing to let go of our outcomes. If we aren't—if we dig our claws in, we risk losing the very things we care enough about to cling to.
All of the tools I need are within me. The heart is the navigator. The consistency I am looking for is me.

I watch myself as a little boy. I am in the backseat of the car. We are driving down the highway and I can see a wolf running alongside, keeping pace effortlessly. He travels with me. He always does.
I am in the kitchen, electricity running through me. My body bouncing up and down. I see the fear and helplessness on my mother's face. I see my father; hoping self preservation will work for him. There is no hesitation. He runs towards me with force and leaps into the air. We both come crashing down on the floor.
I am running through a field. I am talking to someone no one else can see. I am learning things—things that will help me accomplish some great purpose, and I will spend the rest of my life trying to remember what I knew before I lost my childhood in the kitchen.

I am on a sailboat. I can see my human suit lying on the bunk. *My bothers* circles above me, humming softly.
"I can take you now?" a voice begins.
I don't know where the voice is coming from.
"I know you feel alone; abandoned here, like you belong somewhere else.
There is a plan—a kind of master plan, but I can take you now, tonight, in your sleep. It will be like suicide without ever pulling the trigger, and your family won't have to feel like you gave up. They will mourn a different way"
"I just want my life to make sense," I cry.
I have to think about it, afraid to fall asleep before I make a decision.

I am lying on someone's couch, in a basement that is not mine. I am looking up at the rafters and thinking how much I don't want to be here. My vision grows blurry and I find myself in total darkness. I can see the earth in front of me. There are three rings wrapped around the earth, rotating in different directions. *Dreams; Desire; Destiny.* This is the power of creation. The Nogwal. The original source point from which all things are birthed.

I don't know how old I am. I haven't yet learned to walk, but somehow I get out the front door. I make it half way down the hall before my mom discovers I am gone. This is the first time I escape, and my first memory.

I am on the island, on a hill that rises up from the valley. I look around for *my love* but she is not here. The sky grows dark around the pink clouds. Then she speaks. My love speaks to me from somewhere outside of my vision.
"I am here. I never left. I just need to get home, and by home I mean you."
Is it really her speaking, or is it me?
I begin to weep.
"When is this going to stop?" I call out.

My body begins to rise from the hill. A kind of tunnel opens within the pink clouds and I enter into it. Colors swirl around me in the darkness. I am light-headed and disoriented, moving with incredible speed.
Suddenly I am struck with force. It feels like someone has punched me in the stomach. I am back in my body on the floor of the cave. I roll over and can see roots extending from my chest. I can feel energy moving through these roots into me. I hear *my love.*
I turn when I hear you giggle. You are laying next to me. I see a wound on your back and realize it was not my back that was burning, it was yours. It was burning because this whole time I have been journeying, you were connected to me and all the things I was feeling were going into you. *Feeling my experience.*
I pull you close. With my roots connected to your back, we fall asleep on the cave floor, *our bothers* circling above us.

We are traveling through space. To our home in the stars. Me and *my love.* We are joined. We are one. It's impossible to tell whose arms and limbs and legs belong to whom.
We move quickly past stars and planets and colors in many different shapes. We are traveling through a kind of kaleidoscope tunnel. *The psychedelic tunnel.* Images blur into streams around us and in their reflection I can see us sleeping peacefully on the purple bed.

NAVIGATOR

By Home I Mean You

Will my legacy remember me? Having recognized this challenge, will I integrate the lesson I am intended to learn?

"I can't sleep," she begins. "Tell me a story."
"Real or made up?"
"Made up."

One time there was a little boy named Max.
He was very sad and very shy.
One day when his parents were arguing, he ran away.
He ran as fast as he could down country roads and into trees.
He ran through the trees and up and down hills.
He ran like foxes and ducks and scurrying tiny mice.
He ran through rivers and over mountains.
He ran through oceans and through the clouds.
Just to find his way . . .
home.

GOEL

I Can't Even Wait To Get Away From You

We are in the great stone building. There are children everywhere.
Makes perfect sense. She brought them. She is with us.
She has never joined us here. We always come alone.
We walk through the halls and look for her. She has brought the children but she may be an observer, not a participant.
Things are changing, I can feel it. He knows it and I can feel it.
It's not a bad thing, it's just different. They travel in a new way.
He goes to her. He sends his astral body to her, in the land of stone and health and separation.
We pass through the hallways and look for his love; through double doors and walk up stairs into a large open area.

He reacts to something and runs out of the room and back down the stairs. I keep pace with him effortlessly. Maybe he knows where she is, but I don't see *his bothers*, or hers.
Maybe he has heard her call. She talks sometimes from her physical body; calls into this reality. They talk to one another in many different ways.

We are down the stairs and he runs to the door. He presses his face against the glass and looks into the hall. He grips the doorknob tightly and holds it as if preventing someone from entering.
Suddenly we see them. There are two. They appear around a corner and I can see them by looking over his shoulder.
I can feel the tension in him. He spins the deadbolt on the door, frantically. They are getting closer. He gives the door a tug—as if to

test the lock, and the door pulls open. He closes the door and tries the deadbolt again. He gives the door another tug and it swings opens. The lock is not holding.

His panic is intense. He has no idea how to keep them out; to hold back the tide from reaching his love—princess of the timestreams, seamstress of his destiny.

There isn't a moment left to hesitate. One of them has reached the door. Their hand and raggedy sweater smear across the glass. At times like these, all I can do is hope that self preservation will work for him, not against us.

He wakes up in the land of stone and health and separation. It is dark and the house is quiet. I look outside the bedroom door. Someone is coming up the stairs. He watches me and his eyes follow my stare. They are here. He has brought them here. He has brought them from that reality into this one

He leaps out of bed and turns on every light in the house. He brought them with us because he knows they can't survive here. Not without his power. He does everything he can not to give power to her fears.

He turns on every light in the house and begins breathing deeply.

A FORESTS SON, A RIVERS DAUGHTER

Pull Out Your Arsenal

It is sometime in the morning. Traffic has come to a halt and people have wandered onto the streets. They are looking up.
The sky is filled with moons and planets. Ships are coming and going from most of these. They appear to be at war.

Our imminent fear is displaced by the fact that they are fighting one another. It means we have some time to prepare—though I am not sure what we could possibly do in the event of attack.
They seem unaware that we can see them. I think if they knew, they would turn on us at once. They don't know that our eyes have adjusted.
I can't explain why the veil has been ripped away—a veil that has prevented us from observing them.
Somehow I know they have been here for a long time, subtlety posturing the human race, moving the minds of men like the tide moves lava rocks.

I look towards *my love*. She is staring wide eyed into the sky. She looks different. *She always looks the same to me?*
Perhaps it is her luminous body I am now seeing; watching her with my other eyes. I can't understand and don't really try. This is how it works.
As if responding to my resignation, suddenly I know. This is not *my love*. This is *our daughter-God Of The New World*. Hope for all humanity. The one who will restore Priveden. She is my hummingbird.
I follow her gaze back up to the sky, wondering what comes next.

HER FAVORITE

Your Beauty Is As Pure As Tears

I am lying in the snow; a canopy of trees above me. For a moment I think I am back in the Glenn, when I hear *my love* giggle. I turn my head and she is lying beside me. We are making angels in the snow, and we are both proper soaked.
I reach over and brush the soppy hair from her face. She laughs. I close my eyes and softly kiss her.

Time accelerates. We enter the stage doors and walk through the hallways to our dressing room.

Make someone feel like you are not judging them and they are all yours. Restore what has been taken from them by judgement—dignity, self worth and belief in themselves.
Intimacy is authentic communication, no matter what form it takes.
We are attracted to people who represent the things we want, but with love, the attraction remains even if they don't.

If you can't see past how you feel about yourself then you will always find fault in others.
Shift your focus from what others have done *to* you, and start thinking about what you have done to them. What have I done to provoke her into reacting? Because I am only responsible for me; for my ability to respond.
If you can't forgive others, you won't be able to receive forgiveness.

I don't know what the right thing to do is, anymore. I feel completely incapable of making the right decisions. It seems that no matter what I do, I am interpreted through another's filter. No one sees my intention. I think we all just do this to each other.

I open my eyes and you are asleep in my arms. We are in the purple bed, cozy close and tangled together.
I recognize this world, but we are not in the city of stone and health and separation. We are across the Northern Sea from the hill where you gave up your last breath, beyond the borders of that world, in some new life. *The future.*
We are in a cozy little seaside cottage. Our room reminds me of the one we carved into the black rock castle.
On the table beside the bed there is a small jade pyramid.

THE ISLAND

You Are In A Constant State Of Beautiful

I wake up to awareness as we are traveling through the clouds. Me and *my love.*

The moons are full—reflecting off the ocean, lighting our way to the island. We pass through one another with ease. This is what we do. *We are made for this.*

With every touch, a surge of energy flows through me, awakening memories of lives we have shared throughout the timestreams, like a billion photographs passing before my eyes.

I can see us on the black rock castle that towers out of sea in rebellion. We live in a lighthouse across the violent waters from Sinister.

My love has been losing her memories of the timestreams, and this concerns me. It is the reason I have brought us here. I am afraid that if I do not keep her secluded, she will lose the awareness she has left, and I will lose her.

My love spends her days wandering the lighthouse and the black rocks. I can tell she feels alone and abandoned, slowly going mad on this prison I have created for her, while I try and find a way to recall her memories.

We have a purpose, and the time is drawing near to complete what we came here for. Every choice counts, because what we do determines what we have done and what will happen next.

We are travellers on a journey to integrate the heart.

Ahead of us is the Island. We approach with incredible speed. The white sandy beach with the washed up lava rocks, over the jungle that becomes forest and the houses without roofs. We continue across the field to the hill with the stones that stand like a doorway, until we are above the pyramid with ancient symbols.

I can see us in the land of stone and health and separation. I understand that here, too, I treat you like a prisoner to my outcomes.
I suppose the reason we offer ultimatums and conditions on others is because we want to be in control, as if their sole purpose is to fulfil a role in our story that we have designed for them. As if she is the source point for my happiness.

It is threatening when others don't fulfill the roles we have designed for them, because they remind us we are not living in this reality; that our feet are planted in different worlds—ones we have created in our head. It hurts because I have attached myself to a phantom limb that doesn't exist.

The mind is a powerful thing. You don't happen out there—in the world outside yourself. Who you are happens within.
Identity is something you create. Authenticity it is something you are.

NAVIGATOR

Only Where It Take Us

"I just emailed you a picture; an alternate cover for the book. When you have a chance, take a look and let me know what you think. Of course I wouldn't use it unless you are cool with it."

It is early in the morning. I don't expect to hear from *my love* anytime soon. She is sleeping. I can feel it. And when she wakes, she will have things to do. Those things aren't me. I can feel it.

I am beginning to understand what this has been about. By no means a complete understanding, but at least it's something that resembles calm. Besides, if I try to understand, I make this about me—and this is not about me, not completely.
I am remembering so many things, but not enough to feel in control.
Maybe the real learning begins when I stop trying to participate and just let it happen.
My journeys through the timestreams have left me feeling helpless. It is helpless and hopeless I feel when history repeats itself. I don't believe it needs to be this way but as long as I have my claws dug into preferred outcomes, I reinforce the footsteps of my own history. I am more afraid of change than of staying the same, and have paid a price for that.

Life is full of change. It's scary to think the one I depend on the most for the stability I crave, is changing as well. What if she changes away from me?
I believe some greater force guides all of us. I can't decide when to trust and when not to. The moment I try and control, is the moment I risk

losing what has been introduced into my life, and the purpose they are intended to serve. I must accept whatever form others take.
If I have learned anything, this is it. Release. Let go. Reborn.
So new things can birth.

You can't be self aware if you are absent from the now moment, because your ability to respond is hampered by the stories you tell yourself.
We are a society lacking in self awareness, and where you lack self awareness, you lack responsibility for your actions.

Authenticity has become a catch phrase. Ego was never meant to become our identity.
Who was I before the negative belief systems were introduced, before you grew up to believe a story of yourself that was given out like a nickname?
We don't need to invent who we are. We need to un-invent who we have become.
We are not failures, but seekers of a love we feel denied; a love which originates from within. If it didn't, you wouldn't be aware of it, or seeking it.

I imagine life as a river. A river with many currents. Layer upon layer of the same lesson; variations of the same theme.
Sometimes things in life can get lost without the certainty of finding them again. It just may be the universe doing me a favour.

"I just saw the alternate cover. It looks awesome. I'll have to give it some thought."
"I suppose at some point we should ask ourselves if we want people to know this is real or just pass it off as fiction," I respond.

I am taking you to a beautiful valley. It's on the island. And through the trees is the ocean. The moons are full and thunder rolls across the sky like a drum. Lightning divides the sky into flashing puzzle pieces. And we will lie in the grass and I will hold you.

THE ISLAND

The Valley Of Deception

The sky is dark. Flashes of white light illuminate the darkness. The clouds have settled around the moons like a blanket around babies.
I know exactly where we are. There is a kind of map that exists in my head. I know that in front of me is the bluff, separated from the island when the tide comes in. Above is the waterfall, and the volcano.
This island has become my calm between journeys. My consistency. This is where I discover all the answers I am looking for originate from within me.

I hear *her bothers* before I see them both. We walk towards one another and lie down in the grass. I am on my back and *my love* lies on top of me. Our hearts upon one another; our roots relaxed.

What a journey this has been. What a process of learning. Had I been able to control or strategize my way through the timestreams, I would have been less likely to find any peace at all.
Where I am now is in front of me, and I am not alone. I have *my love.* She may seem to change as often as the desert gets storms, but the destination is the same. She is always here. Always with me, as I am always with her.
Moving within the flow of the timestreams is the path of destiny; the channel of the Divine.

She is sleeping peacefully on my chest. I don't want to wake her so I roll outside of my body. There is something I need to do. *A call.*
I turn to her. I reach my hand out and follow the curves of her face. *I have learned so much from you, my love. I have learned* how *to love you.*

I close my eyes and softly kiss her.

I appreciate walking through trees at night. The jungle or the forest, it doesn't matter. Shadows cast long, obscuring my view of things and wrapping me in darkness. There is a layer of eerie to the experience. It's unnerving. I can't see a thing. Rocks could be in front of me or beasts lying in wait. It is one of the few places where one can truly feel at peace and calm and panic.

With the ocean rolling in the distance and the openness of the valley behind me, I easily fall from the arms of sweet deception.
I jump across the rocks to reach the bluff—slowly separating itself from the island.
It's like an amputated limb, destined to rejoin the body after the great exhale.

From my place on the rocks I gaze down into the water. A flash of white lights up the sky like a puzzle piece. Forest shadows have followed me. They lurk in the darkness across the water.
Thunder echoes the divine drum.
I think of *my love* sleeping peacefully on my tired and rusty human suit. How precious she is. *How precious she has become.* We journey together. We travel the timestreams as twin flames; a mutual agreement to remind one another why we are here.
And why are we here? Have I figured this out?
I am here to learn how to love authentically. That's all I know.

It's taken a long time to discover my peace. It is authentic because it can't be lost. It can't be lost because it comes from within me.
If tonight is the last time *my love* asks me to come to her—to hold and comfort her, then when tomorrow comes, a new future comes with it. Every end is a beginning. The power is within me. Why would I give that away?

Authentic love is not finding your identity in a story of someone else you have to embellish to stay interested. Authentic love is refusing the story and embracing the now moment, with all its natural beauty and charm.

Love is not concerned with time—with things past or things to come. Love lives in the present, and in the present moment is love.

The sky flashes white and as it does I look down into the water. I see my reflection, only it's not what I expect.

When I wake up in the morning, I'm still sleeping by your side.

THE DESERT

He Closed His Eyes And Softly Kissed Her

I am wandering through the desert. *Egypt.*
Where is my love. *Safe.*
Where am I going? *To her.*

Despite the sandstorm, I am not worried. I am not worried because some things are inevitable. I am on my way to her. This is who we are. This is what we were made for.
Life is full of sandstorms. They cloud our sight but the destination remains the same. Eventually the storm will pass. The sun will come out again, and when it does, the only damage done will be what we have created by panicking.

In the midst of the storm, it is easy to get off course—especially when we panic. We panic because we are not in control.
If we start wandering about, we create separation. The best thing to do in a storm is hunker down and let it pass, but that makes us feel powerless and there is a belief system that suggests that if you don't try and manipulate circumstance than you are indifferent, gutless, lacking confidence or a coward. I am not any of those things.
Why would I want to wander around in this storm and get myself all turned around?
Letting go is tough. It's like amputating an arm that never existed but you have allowed yourself to believe was essential.

I follow GOEL to a cave, tucked into a black rock castle, spit out of the desert in rebellion. It is time to hunker down and wait out the storm.

I fall asleep listening to the howling wind beat against this desert fortress.

When I close my eyes, I sleep. When I sleep, I dream.
I am in the white room. The one with twin doors without handles. The door on the roof has gone. The old wooden chair has been replaced with the purple bed. I move towards the bed and lie down, but my mind is too awake to sleep. I want to know why I have come here. I get up and walk towards the wall. When I touch it, the white paint begins to peel away. A dark wood is exposed, inlaid with jade stones. As I walk along the walls, the wake of my hand leaves streaks of the surface underneath.
Suddenly I find myself standing in front of a door. I never saw it before. Maybe only because my eyes are still adjusting.
It is an old wooden door. It reminds me of the chair that is usually here, but things are changing, and change isn't always a bad thing.
There are many scratches on the door. Symbols and writing. Geometric etchings. My fingers slide along the grooves, as if this will allow me to experience the essence of who placed them here. And for what reason.

I hear a voice behind me. Above and behind me. A voice from outside this dream. "Mark! Look at me! Look at me! Look at me!"
It is the voice of *my love* when she is singing the lullaby, only she is speaking.
I wake up on my logical side. I wake up lifting my head in response to *my love*, but she is not here.
The storm is over. I am alone in the cave with GOEL. He is awake. I am never able to wake before him.
We walk to the cave entrance. The sandstorm is over. The sun is shining and the future is bright.

THE LOST GOSPEL

Consider This Your Debt Repaid

I walk out of the cave. I am midway up a very steep and rocky plateau that overlooks a body of water and a great valley.
I am dressed in a light cloth wrapped around my body. This isn't Egypt anymore.

There are fishing boats in the water below, returning with their early morning catch. I can see my wife. She has gone down to bargain for our early meal.
She turns and looks up at the Qumran. Our eyes meet. This is not *my love*. This is my wife.
I step away from the entrance to the cave and begin climbing the rocks. When I reach the top, I walk along a path. I stop underneath a great tree. There is a boulder I sit on and wait.

Time accelerates and he is sitting in front of me. This man is my childhood friend, and my teacher. He is a master.
We have been meeting this way for years. Early in the morning. We talk of philosophy, politics and spirituality.
Sometimes he wanders in the surrounding desert alone and takes refuge in the caves where I live, with my wife and our community. He is always welcome amongst us. He has been my friend since we were children.

When childhood outgrows us, the ideas of young boys develop into the ideas of men.
Those ideas rarely look the way we imagined, and sometimes don't even resemble one another.

As children, we often spoke of becoming great leaders of a revolution; a revolution to overthrow the forces that occupy us. Instead, I married prematurely and live in a cave, but in my own way, I am living out a version of that childhood dream. And in a way, so is he.
When his father became ill, my friend took over the responsibility for the family business and providing for his mother and siblings. Not long ago he passed on that responsibility to his brother, and left the business—and his family, behind.
He speaks of revolution but his ideas of how to accomplish this have changed. He doesn't fight with weapons. He speaks of love.

I don't love my wife the way I should. I don't love her completely. She is aware of this, and when she looks at me—like she did this morning, she reminds me that she knows.
My heart is divided.

"What are you seeking?" he asks me.
"A life that is not controlled by outside forces," I respond.
"Good luck," he responds and we both laugh.

We often speak of matters of the heart. Actually, you might say we always do. My friend gently reminds me that control is not what I should be seeking. That if we set ourselves to control the world around us, we will never be satisfied; that there is a universal river that flows and all we can expect from trying to establish control, is disappointment and frustration. He reminds me that every choice counts.
"Your only choice is to react or respond to your human experience," he continues.

"How is it that you do not return her faithfulness?" he asks.
There are layers to his words. He refers to my divided heart. My conviction of purpose *and* the other woman.
I have spent most of my life believing that I was missing something that would make me feel complete, and this continues to drive me to seek answers outside of myself; answers I feel are currently unavailable to me because of choices I have made. I find myself resenting my wife, as though she is what prevents me from becoming the person I want to be.

I want to be a part of the revolution. I want to make a difference in the world around me. I want to change it.

"The vineyards that yield the best grapes are the ones watered regularly. Do you understand? You can spend your whole life trying to transform was is not yours to change into an image that mimics what you desire. Even if you succeed, it will only be an illusion. Or you can embrace what is in front of you; what already is."

My wife does not relate to my conviction of purpose. She is a wonderful woman, completely satisfied to fulfill her role as wife and mother. She longs for nothing else, and I wish she did. I wish I could speak to her of greater things—of the world beyond this world, but she has no interest.

When we made the decision to leave the city and form our own community, my wife was reluctant. She was not eager to abandon the things she had grown accustom to. Progress was making our civilization great, and would make it mythical. She could not understand my reasons.
I have made life hard for her. We live in this rocky fortress because it exists outside of what others have come to accept as normal; beyond the immediate reach of corrupt religious and political systems that govern the cities and towns around us.

Had she not been as loyal and sweet as she is, our marriage would surely have ended. Perhaps there was a part of her that hoped—even expected, that I would change. Now I wonder if she resents herself for loving someone who does not love her the way she loves.
I don't know why she stays with me. I have increasingly withdrawn from her. The best part of intimacy is communication—in whatever form that takes, and we don't communicate the way we once did. I am not certain that the woman I married was anything more than a story I told myself.
As layers of my own wilful delusion are stripped away, I can no longer support the life I built for myself. Or perhaps I have simply lost the desire to.
Will I try and redeem this situation or discard it?

Often the ones we love end up being the ones we put the most effort into manipulating. We don't want to be lonely. We allow people to become routines, even when they no longer serve our highest and greatest good.
Life is full of change. It's scary to think the ones we depend on the most for the stability we crave, are changing as well.
I feel like a coward for trying to prompt her into discarding me. It just seems easier than making the decision on my own.

"When you make decisions strategically—thinking you can anticipate how she will react, your only success is to embody the very feeling you are trying to manipulate. Your self-preservation works against you. Your inner turmoil is eating you up."
He is right, of course. I wonder where I went so wrong.
"Change yourself, and others will change because they see change in you. This is the power of influence; but never imagine you can predict the how they will change."

He speaks in layers, not riddles, because the experience of life is multidimensional.
"There is no need to contemplate what you know, just act upon it. If you listen with your heart instinctively, you will know what is right for you, and you will integrate the lessons you are intended to learn. Your conviction of purpose will be relieved, and knowledge will not have corrupted you."

Time accelerates. My wife has died. I am quick to marry the other woman. This brings me no more happiness than my first marriage, because it was an impulsive decision to satisfy my increasing disorientation.
Not long after she died, my friend was killed. His message threatened too many people. He was a mirror in a land of people who don't appreciate seeing their own reflection.

I find myself consumed with grief over the loss of my first wife; for what I neglected to say and do. When change—even change we desire, is initiated by a force outside of ourselves, we quickly come to feel powerless.

I often contemplated my life without her in it, but now that she is gone, I can't stop thinking about how good I had it; how perfect she was. *I could have loved her more.*
As I relive these lost opportunities in my head, the more I torment myself with my inability to change the past.
I realize how much I hurt her and these visions plague my memories. Taking her away from her friends and family—isolating her in the desert, I believed it was the right thing to do, and I assumed it was right for her.
We lived here happily and we lived here miserably. On a moment by moment basis, with moment by moment pain. The kind of pain that eats you alive from the inside. The kind of pain that lies.

I believe it was her broken heart that killed her. Her divided heart. She was tired, and felt alone.
We felt the same way and somehow I never saw that. I refused to see it. My eyes never adjusted to what was right in front of me. My ears never adjusted to her frequency. If they had, I would have realized I was exactly where I needed to be.

I don't know what to do. *I don't know what will happen next.* I whisper the words as tears roll from my eyes.
I am consumed with fear that my actions will prevent me from ever finding the happiness I have spent my life searching for, as if a great chasm now exists. Eternally separated from all that had been given to me; from what I needed most.
My stomach churns, as though eating itself.

I mourn because I am not with her; that the opportunity to share this life together has been taken from me. I am consumed with regrets. Regrets that remind me that I am responsible for what I do; that every choice counts, and how things in life—people we love and who love us, can get lost without the certainty of ever finding them again.
The body is designed to mourn, I know this. All of the tools to navigate through the experience of life are contained within us, and I don't believe that mourning must be a kind of terrible suffering.
Somehow I can't resolve intellectual knowledge with how I feel, and knowledge that is not applied, destroys. It destroys us because discarding

what we have learned is a gesture towards complacency, reflecting our stubbornness to change.

My second wife is very different. When I began to fall into her eyes, we were very much alike. It seemed that way, but when the master was killed, she gave up. She regressed into a kind of hopelessness after she realized there was a cost to the change she desired. Hopelessness offers her comfort because she is more afraid of change than she is of staying the same.

"You think you are the only one in pain?" I ask her.

She is rooted in belief systems that have led her to believe that her life is intended to be miserable; or doomed to be.

We are attracted to people who represent the things we want. I don't love my second wife. I like her, but that's not the same. I am not even attracted to her anymore.

I don't think she loves me, either. We simply made a mutual agreement against loneliness.

One day I ask her to kill me.

We rise early one morning, quieter than usual so we don't wake anyone. We walk down to where the fishing boats have not yet returned.

"Don't stop even if I struggle," I instruct her.

She didn't need to be here. I could have done this myself though I am not sure I would have the strength. I need her for this. I needed to give her this. Perhaps the action of holding me down will empower her, allowing her to live the rest of her life in peace; with some new strength.

I don't know if I believe that, but I need to believe something, because sometimes the belief of a thing is better than an absolute.

Lying here—looking up through the water at this woman who I never really loved, all I can think of is that I have let her down, as well. Completing the cycle I have lived my entire life. Always looking for some greater alternative, perpetually discovering there is none. Because things flourish where you water them.

I thought I could release myself from this prison of my own making, but I only succeeded in dying with the knowledge that I was not the person I thought I was.

"What did your heart tell you to do today, and did you listen?"
"It told me to let go of someone, and I did."

NAVIGATOR

Are You Feeling Better Now

"I can't imagine it would be a good thing for your relationship if we passed the book off as anything but fiction."
"I was going to ask you to keep the cover clear of my face."
"No problem. I made that mostly for me, but wanted you to see it."
"I loved it. It's awesome. Thanks for understanding. You are so lovely."
"Time to start living in this reality. I am tired of trying to try and live in them all. And I have discovered I don't have to."
"Yea, it's exhausting bouncing all around in different consciousnesses and realities."

"I wouldn't actually want you involved if you were not authentically interested. It was a fun thought for a moment—doing promotion together and all that, but this is getting much bigger. With the music coming up and there's even talk of a film."
"If that opportunity arises, we will talk. This is your book."
"My book, our story. Why would you be more open to being involved at a later point? It's not going to do your relationship any favours then, either—and you will have to deal with then, what you are trying to avoid now."
"What am I avoiding?"
"Just having people around you know this is real. That's all I meant. I'm not judging you for that. Fair enough. It would change things, and change is not always what people want. I am pretty indifferent at this point—to be honest."
"What?"
"I can understand why you wouldn't want people to know it was you."
"Okay. I like being anonymous."
"The actress likes being anonymous—ha! I call bullshit."

"Yeah. I don't know."
"I think maybe you are just waiting to see if it's going to be worth it. It's like a gamble for you. You know it will cost you something to reveal the truth."
"I haven't even read it, yet. I have to read before I decide."
"And you will. I hope to get your comments before it goes to the publisher, but not sure you want to be that involved. There is a fine line between peace and apathy. At some point, I am not going to care if you want to be involved. It won't matter cause it doesn't need you."
"Okay."

"No matter what you do, your decisions write this book. They always have and they will write the sequel. Your decisions here affect what happens through the timestreams. Every choice counts."
"That makes me so excited."

THE ONE THEY CALL THE VISION

You Know When You'll Be Forgiven

I am descending through a canopy of trees into the clearing between the doorways where faeries enter this world. A layer of snow causes the green beneath it to shimmer.

His hair is wet. His hands are bloody. In one of them, he holds his lost manhood, and when he breathes his last, the muscles atrophy.

ANU'U

AM I IN ANY WAY DIVINE?

I am standing in an elevator. It's ascending. 136. 225. 297. 333. 365. The elevator has stopped. Ok, I guess this is it. I guess this is my floor.

I step outside the elevator into a large room unlike anything I have ever seen. The walls are a dark wood, inlaid with jade stones. Large panoramic windows stretch around the entire room.
Something about here feels very familiar to me.

I move towards the window on my left. Outside there is a field covered in snow. *The field where we bury the bodies standing up.* I turn around and look across the room, at the window opposite. Oceans Gate, and the black rock castle spit out of the sea in rebellion.
Through the window at the front of the room is the purple bed, in the land of stone and health and separation. *My love* is mostly asleep. I walk closer, my fingers trace the geometric symbols in the wood.

"Until what happens in your head is experientially greater than what happens outside of it, you will not be fully integrated."
I spin around and see a woman sitting in a white leather chair. She wasn't there when I got off the elevator, but I don't question this stuff anymore. Next to her is a small table with an antique radio on it, a pot of tea, and a small jade pyramid.
I walk over to her.
"Is this it? Is this the end? And now I can return home."
"Don't imagine you know where—or who, home is," she replies.
Instantly I feel as though I have betrayed myself; like I confessed my attachment to an outcome. I have so many questions, but my questions make this about me, and it's not about me—not completely.

"Have a seat," she continues. "I have brewed us some tea."
A matching white chair has materialized behind me. I sit down, excited to be moving forward; progressing.

"You carry the light of where you came from," she begins. "Your journeys have revealed to you the cyclical nature of patterns. What you do now will determine what has been done, which is why you began. Do you understand?"
"I am not sure," I reply. "Are you saying that all of the things I experienced are in the past?"
She shakes her head.
"It's not that simple. Time is not measured linearly within the timestreams. What you have experienced is happening side by side—simultaneously, and is still happening. This is why your actions in one reality become reactions in the next."
"Like mimicry," I offer, eager to impress upon her that I have learned something. She smiles politely, and I understand that my understanding is crude, at best.
"Because you experience time as a steady consistent progression," she continues, "you tend to think of events as organically flowing and unpredictably fluid. However, time does not work that way. You are simply moving through space too slowly to gain the proper perspective."

"Time must be dissolved. The frequency that it carries as humanity evolves is separating them from the Divine.
Time has begun folding in on itself. Now is the time of progression; a progression to the point of stillness we call the zero point or—as you have understood it, the source point, from which original creation is birthed. From this point of stillness, something completely new is birthed. This is where your concept of mimicry falls short.
History is not doomed to repeat itself. This is a negative belief system that keeps people waiting for a glitch in the pattern instead of taking the incentive to be the change they are looking for.
Self awareness sheds light on how experience has shaped identity; an identity based on stories that influence how you interact with the world. This is the point of stillness from which reinvention is possible."

"I look forward to thinking differently," I respond. I don't doubt her words, I just lack the application which makes it real, and integrates a new belief system.

"The book you have been writing carries your essence, and it dissolves time. It resonates from the pause between breaths, and will guide humanity towards the zero point. This is inevitable. Nothing can intervene.
Eight cosmic keys will be given to you. The keys represent new doorways to even greater possibilities for humanity and the cosmos.
You must stand in the energy of grace for self. You will find divine truth in tears. This is essential to the process of love awareness. It is in this duality that you will understand yourself and discover how to proceed on this journey."
"So it has not come to an end?" I ask.
"No," she responds, "but don't let that frustrate you. Every moment—every word, is a constant state of beginning. If you look for an ending, all the opportunities in front of you will pass without you ever noticing."
"But what of *my love*?
"She is your light partner. Your longing for her is your desire to be reunited with the family you left behind. This is your endeavour to be home."
"My family?"
"Yes, your wife and daughter."
"Are you suggesting *my love* is on this journey with me, or did I leave her behind?"
"I can't tell you that."
"Is *my love* simply a manifestation of what I desire, a kind of archetype?"
The Anu'u doesn't respond.

"It was essential that you enter the timestreams without any knowledge of who you were before. It is the only way you can have an authentic human experience. I will confirm to you only things that are permissible, when they become relevant."
She puts her tea down and somehow I know that our conversation is drawing to a close.

"Listen to the song that's being sung in their wings. This is the frequency that will guide you to the answers you are looking for.
In addition to the keys, you will discover an emerald tablet. It contains the location of the keys."
"What do I do with the keys?"
"They will integrate into you. You will feel them in your wrists. She will feel them in her ankles."

SATORI

The Wanting Comes In Waves

I am sitting in the white room, on the old wooden chair. An antique radio sits on a small table in front of me. They have both aged.
The radio sizzles to life with a surge.

Behind the static I hear a voice. A voice I recognize. I stretch forward and adjust the dial until I can hear it clearly.
I can picture the person in my head as they speak. Their words convey feeling; a language different than how they speak.
As they continue, I can't help feeling voyeuristic, like I am eavesdropping.
I feel a bit guilty so I reach forward and adjust the dial.

I don't have to turn far before I hear a different voice clearly. I remember this conversation, though what I am hearing is so much more detailed than the words that were used. I can even pick out the parts they verbalized, and I am overwhelmed by how much they didn't—even to the point of neglecting their true feelings.

I understand vulnerabilities. It's why we protect ourselves. It is why we choose our words, even if we don't mean them; even if we just want to insinuate ideas and provoke others to think a certain way.
A lack of honesty is a breach in honesty. There is a belief system which would disagree with me; a belief system that separates honesty from deceit. I don't know how that works, or how people can accept that.
Insinuation is manipulation. When we make decisions based on how we anticipate others to think and react, we cause ourselves to feel the way we intended them to.

I adjust the dial until I hear another voice. Again, this is someone I recognize immediately. They are also sharing their feelings; pouring out their insecurities. It seems so unnatural for them to be sharing like this. I continue to adjust the dial and every frequency seems to be another voice; another heartfelt confession.

I made a decision to enter the timestreams if for no other reason than a great conviction of purpose. I need to trust that decision. I would rather do the right things then spend my life trying to understand them. It is the only way to progress.
Any burden too big is not a result of failure, but of choice. I should focus more on what I ought to do, not what I am capable of doing.
I believe all the tools I need to complete this journey are within me.

I can spend our whole life seeking answers and never progress, or I can endeavour to know and embrace the responsibility that comes with knowledge.
Knowledge you refuse to put into use has the power to corrupt. This is what it means to integrate the lessons we go through life learning.

Emotion can navigate without thinking. Fear is like a magnet on the compass. It makes things tougher. It introduces logic as a substitute for what we intuitively know.

I find it quite natural to tune into the frequency of others. It is my self righteousness that makes me feel entitled. When I make my gifts about me, I make everything about me.

Relationships are tools to help us get back in our own body; into the now moment. The freedom to learn from one another is the pillar upon which successful relationships are built.
There will always be challenges because there is not a person you will ever meet who will act exactly as you would. And when others act differently, we feel threatened. When others let us down, I often surrender my dignity to them.

If everyone fixed themselves, the world would fix itself.

Suddenly it hits me, like a wave. A voice from within.
You won't feel loved until someone can tune into your frequency.

NAVIGATOR

We Will Roll Like River Stones

"You know what's nice? Not fighting with you. We haven't bickered in a long time. And it's nice."
"I feel the same way. It's so beautiful; the way it is meant to be. We are not meant to fight and argue. We are meant to love each other, and the biggest obstacle to authentic love is ego."

"I just woke up from a dream about you. I don't remember it, but there is a tune in my head; the tune our bothers hum. The song they sing with their wings."

HER FAVORITE

A Cozy Seaside Cottage

I am walking through a field. It is drizzling. In front of me is the sea. I know that somewhere behind me is the cozy seaside cottage—the one that reminds me of the home we carved out of the black rock castle; the one I woke up to on the purple bed, with *my love* and the jade pyramid on the bedside table.
I have paid a price to be here. That price is not something to be mourned. The only burden on my shoulders is accepting the cost of decisions I have made.

It feels like mid morning. I look around for *my love*. I am alone in the field, but I can feel her close. Her essence surrounds me. I can reach out and feel it whenever I need to. And when I do, a surge goes through my body and I feel healed. Happy and healed. Happy, healed, and rejuvenated.
The wind is singing. I feel the earth beneath me. The water rages in front of me. The fire is within.

The one thing you appreciate with age is time. Every moment of your life that isn't your own is a moment you have given away.
There is a difference between loneliness and being alone. Sometimes I wonder if my self-preservation has done more to prevent me from happiness than it has faithfully to guide me into it, but this is only because I was looking outside of myself to be complete. I know this now. I can change things. *I am changing.*

When I leave my body and join together with *my love*—wrapped together in a blanket of peace and calm, I find all the contentment I have ever longed for. All the hopes of many lifetimes unite into an expression of ecstasy that no words can adequately describe.

I am walking through this field. It is raining lightly and suddenly I am outside of my body. I am standing in front of me, with my back towards the ocean, watching the physical me.
"The best thing I ever did was love you."
She drops out of the sky behind him. *My love.* He doesn't see her yet.

THE ISLAND

YOU CAN STAY AS LONG AS YOU LIKE

I am sitting in the crystal blue water. My legs are nearly covered, but not quite. *My love* stands behind me, pouring water over me and massaging it into my skin.
I don't know how long this lasts. It doesn't matter because I am so calm and relaxed.
I feel like an observer, even though I am in my body.

There is a flash in the sky, as if time has just accelerated and I am missing frames. *My love* is gone and there is a jade tablet between my legs, as high as my chest. It is covered in strange symbols that I recognize, but am unable to read—at least until my eyes adjust.
I look through the haze created by heat and see a light shining out of the water, about twenty feet away from me.
I am so relaxed that I don't want to stand. I don't even know if I can. I am so dizzy because my spirit hasn't fully connected with my body.
I roll onto my knees and begin crawling towards the light.

I reach into the water where the light is, and find a key. A jade key. Then I notice another light shining through the water. I feel a bit more strength than I had, but continue on my hands and knees towards it.
I find another jade key, and see another light ahead.

By the time I have retrieved the eighth key, I have rounded the bend of the island. A whirlwind of water rises out from the ocean. I am on my feet, now, and approach it cautiously. The closer I get, the more confident I become that I am intended to enter it.

I am standing in the snow somewhere in the mountains. In a valley between peaks. In front of me is a large owl. Bigger than any I have ever seen, even in pictures. The owl is taller than half the size of me.
I have no fear, but I am in awe. Respectful awe. I am content to just share this moment without speaking. When the time is right for words, I will know it.

He speaks without words. This owl is wisdom and it wants to know what it can do for me.
"Can you be with *my love*? Just be with her and help her know what to do; what is the highest and greatest good, cause I don't know what is right for her and don't want to presume I do."
The moment I finish speaking my wrist clicks. I didn't do anything to provoke this. My arm was entirely relaxed, and suddenly I remember what the Anu'u told me.
"They will integrate into you. You will feel them in your wrists."
Does this mean I have the first key? I want to ask, but don't vocalize it.

The owl turns and spreads his wings. He launches into the air and I find myself traveling with him. Suspended between his wings. We soar above the valley and into a snowstorm.
Now I recognize where we are. We are flying towards the field where we bury our dead standing up. We are flying towards the cave of my consciousness, where *my love* is hunkered down inside. *Waiting for me.* I wonder what she has discovered about me while in there. My excitement grows, knowing we will soon be reunited.

Letting go is one of the hardest things we will ever do—and one of the most painful, which makes it one of the most important things we can ever learn.
We have a collection of attitudes we believe about ourselves. These beliefs become the zero point of our power; they become our destiny.

Fear postures us to impose our will on the future. By transcending learned experience, by stepping out of it—as an observer, you can progress through firsthand knowledge, to freedom.

Freedom is looking at yourself vulnerably, and admitting that you have been living a story you told yourself, unable to resolve why the life you are living is not the one you imagine.
This is how I realized that *my love* was the one who saved me.

There were ghosts, and the ghosts became standards by which all new experiences were filtered. Filters—like belief systems, produce inevitable outcomes. Outcomes I did not desire but my self-preservation believed were essential to protect me. Anything that threatened those outcomes was sabotaged, reinforcing the footsteps of my history.

My love found a way to get through to me. She taught me to appreciate that I was part of a bigger picture, and that bigger picture is not just about me. She became the archetype I needed to see myself—embodying the love that originates from within me and the love I constantly seek from outside. And she freed me from the prison of my own making.

Creation is the art of letting go. The price of knowledge is the responsibility to use it. Authentic love does not originate from a source outside of ourselves, it comes from within. Until we learn to love ourselves apart from the dependency we place on others for validation and identity, we will never find what we actually need—the completeness that comes from recognizing our purpose, and walking in it.
My love showed me how love, by teaching me how to love her.

We leave the cave when the storm is over. We climb out amidst puzzle pieces that have assembled into a mountain, as if a giant came along and put them together again.

You are the pilot.

There is no time left for excuses. YOU are the change you are looking for. TODAY is the NOW MOMENT. Don't delay.
In this life, we have the best life we ever had.

NOGWAL

The Sparks Flew Up To Heaven

We were in space. We could pass through one another.
We were flying from star to star, leaving a trail of light behind us that connected the stars like a constellation.
And everything made sense.

Epilogue

Last night I went to *my love*. She didn't ask me. She never had the chance. I went to my love and found her on the purple bed.
I am not sure she wanted me to come, not all of her. Not the her residing in this world of stone and health and separation, which I have come to realize is the reality I started from, and the one I must stay.

Love is not about letting go, it's about being willing to; but sometimes it is about letting go. You can't hold back the tide, and you can't help someone who won't help themselves, not really. Enabling others to continue without taking incentive and empowering them to change are very different things. No amount of your belief in others will change them. The most you can hope for is to inspire, because eventually, they must believe in themselves
It comes down to choice. The decisions we make determine our priorities, and our priorities reveal where the heart authentically resides.

Resistance creates barriers to progress, and I have come too far on my journeys through the timestreams to stop here.
When every cell in my body is telling me one thing, then to not listen, would be to disrespect the process that brought me to this point.
One of the hardest things we will ever experience is letting go. It is an art form that has only been mastered by the Divine, and only from within this channel of authentic love can we discover how to let go with grace and a kind of dignity that allows for the reinvention of a thing.

I arrive in front of my sleeping princess, filled with the sensation of mourning. It's not a sad kind of mourning because I am not mourning for me. I am grieving for her.

It has taken me a long time to discover my peace. It is authentic because it can't be lost. It can't be lost because it comes from within me.
I walk past her jelly bean toes and stand above her head. I reach out and place my hand on her third eye.
"It is time, *my love*. It's time to go."
The energy that once flowed through her is a memory I hold in my mind, like a photograph. I imagine the wind lightly blowing through her tangled mess of hair. She is beautiful.
A kind of residue passes into my palm. It climbs my arms and wraps itself tightly around my bones, just below the shoulders. This is where my tension is stored. This is my tension relieved.
She has a look on her face. I have seen it before, in this reality and many like it. *Why have I been abandoned? Why am I trapped here?*

How quickly everything changed. One moment the entire world seems yours for the taking and then next—it still is. The only thing keeping us from realizing this is the story we tell ourselves that all good things come to an end. Good things don't end, they just transition. Our challenge is to keep pace, and try to do it as effortlessly as possible.

Sometimes those we love most get lost without the surety of ever finding them again. No amount of wilful delusion can restore the passing of time or hold back the tide of progress.
If I have to embellish reality to stay interested, I will remain a prisoner of my own stories, unable to resolve why the world I live in is not the one I imagine it should be, searching for a way to live calmly inside the chaos I have created for myself. Truth will never be given an opportunity to manifest because I am too caught up in what does not exist, and perhaps never did.

I am not the same person I was when this journey began. As her essence escapes the human suit, I am greeted by *my love—her higher self.* I tell her that I know she did her best and I knew when she could not go on. I tell her that I will take her to GOEL—the gift of everlasting love. I will take her there and then I must come back because I believe in a plan—a kind of master plan, and I am only beginning to learn what that may be. And when tomorrow comes, a new future comes with it. Every end is a new beginning.

This is going to be fun.

The difference between loneliness and being alone, do you understand now? Being alone is a choice. While it is not a choice I make from desire, it is a choice I make out of necessity—for now, because my self preservation is lurking about like a lion in the shadows of darkness.

After Word

Mark and I have been close friends for the better part of 5 years. Sometimes deeply connected, other times not. Several months before *Regressions* manifested itself through him, Mark flipped me a text after I'd tried apologizing for disengaging from our friendship for a time. *"I believe in leaving space for friends to be human."*

That message had a profound affect on me. The lack of judgement in it. The sincere friendship it points too. The appreciation, acceptance and respect for who I authentically am. Mostly though, I heard love. My actions didn't have to match his story of what a friend 'should act like'. Mark could accept the quirks and merits of my unique version of friendship.

If any meaningful, truly intimate relationship can be reduced to a single lesson or mantra or statement—and I don't think it's possible, the message he sent would be it— "I believe in leaving space for friends to be human." It was more than just a message to me personally, it was a prescient of the remarkable transition about to take place within him, and it underscores every layer of *Regressions*, as revealed in the subtitle, *The lengths people will go to discover authentic love.*

So how did this journey to the discovery of authentic love come about?

In late February 2012, Mark and I were at a local tea house for the first time since a busy beginning to the new year. When we sat down, he couldn't contain his excitement. "Life is so amazing!" was his response to my "How are you?"

While I have always found Mark to be articulate, realistic and straight-shooting, the person in front of me was nothing short of effervescent

"Old ghosts are letting go. I am on a new path of self discovery that is helping me make sense out of what seemed like the random events of my life. This makes me feel like there is a point. And it's healing. That's what I'm experiencing; I'm being healed!"

When I pressed him for details, he shared insights, synchronicities and fantastic stories—many of which are contained in this book, of love and one remarkable connection that was changing his life.

During our friendship I've seen Mark lit-up over ideas, but I'd never seen this before. There was a combination of clarity, enthusiasm and complete confidence that from within the passion he could hardly contain, a book would emerge that would inspire others.

And there was something else different about him. I can't say I'd seen it before, or rather, I don't remember seeing it. As he spoke, Mark was operating from a state of gratitude. Profound gratitude. Not just for the healing he was receiving, but for everything he'd experienced to get here, as though every event of his life had become a puzzle piece and he was beginning to put the bigger picture together.

While I don't think I'd recognize an enlightened person, I've done enough searching to know that his gratitude was probably indicative of a spiritual awakening of some kind. He'd seen, felt or gone through something he couldn't undo. And in turn, that something was undoing the Mark I thought I knew. More importantly it was undoing the Mark *he* knew.

Over the next few months, *Regressions* became a canvas for Mark, upon which he could visualize his life and discover how to write the destiny he wanted. In the process, the past was letting go of him, and as such, a transformation took place. He was different. Very different.

The best part is Mark was already a very different person to begin with. That's what had initially attracted me to our friendship. I'd never met anyone who only worked as much as he needed to live. Since I've known him, work has only ever been a means to living—living to create art. Never more so than now.

In *Regressions,* Mark has found his message. He is living it and now he wants us to join him there in the space where the past is toothless, where authentic love can be discovered and where friends can be human.

I, for one, am eager to meet him there; but mostly I'm thrilled Mark is leading the charge.

Les Mottosky, July 2012

CONTINUE THE ADVENTURE

PROGRESSIONS

I will tell you about the time I met a ladybug.

It happened in the garden. I was a little boy at that time, dressed in my woolly blue coat that made me look like Paddington Bear. My hair was swooped to the side like one of the Beatles, from the early years.

The grass was especially high that year due to the heavy rains that greeted spring. It had been a long winter and the snow had nowhere to go, so everything flooded out.
I was wearing my yellow gumboots, on account of mud.

In the garden were large flowers, about as towering as I was high. It was easy to get lost in there. In fact, this was pretty routine for me. I had this fascination with getting lost, actually. Is that weird?

No, I did, as well.

The garden out back was one of my favourite places to escape to. I always had the best adventures in there, was the greatest of heroes, and knew the loveliest princess.

A Princess?!

Yes, Princess Ambellina, but this is a story about the time I met a ladybug. Don't worry, this was no ordinary ladybug. It was the size of *your bothers*, for one thing.

As I was saying, the grass was towering above me like jungle trees. I could taste the smell of heat and hear the crystal blue water tumble down on the white sandy beach.

KeyGen